The Alpha's Principal-Kissed Omega

By

Lorelei M. Hart

Copyright

The unauthorized reproduction or distribution of a copyrighted work is illegal. Criminal copyright infringement, including infringement without monetary gain, is investigated by the FBI and is punishable by fines and federal imprisonment.

Editor Wizards in Publishing
Cover design by Fantasia Frog Designs
Published by Decadent Publishing LLC

The Alpha-Kissed Series by Lorelei M. Hart

The Alpha's Autumn-Kissed Omega

The Alpha's Candy-Kissed Omega

The Alpha's Cranberry-Kissed Omega

The Alpha's Santa-Kissed Omega

The Alpha's Ginger-Kissed Omega

The Alpha's Lifeguard-Kissed Omega

The Alpha's Principal-Kissed Omega

Coming Soon!

The Alpha's Biker-Kissed Omega

All I hoped for was a quiet life teaching in a small town...
But the first few days spent in a motel left me feeling ungrounded, and the assignment to teach omega studies had me considering running back to the big city for fear of letting a bunch of kids down. Could I do justice to the subject?

Then Principal Armison walked into my classroom, offered to rent me the apartment above his garage, and, while he offered to be no more than my principal and my landlord, I hoped this alpha would also see we were destined to be mates. Because I knew we were with every fiber of my being.

But this principal was far more than just an academic. When he left school every day he donned leathers and hopped on his motorcycle to ride to Principal Ink...his tattoo shop, barber shop, and biker social club.

I was starting to feel like I was in over my head, but in such a good way. He was all my fantasies rolled into one. And with every day we spent together, I saw more of why he'd make such a great partner in life and, sooner than I ever dreamed, father of the child I was carrying.

Chapter One

Henry Coastal

A first day in a new school was always nerve-racking. And a first day in a new school in a new town where I knew almost nobody? Enough to send me into a tailspin. But after the breakup, I just couldn't face seeing him...either of them...every day at work.

So, I put feelers out and was lucky enough to find a position mid-year, which I snapped up. The fact my new job was in a small town had actually been a negative, but one I was willing to look past. Parking my car in the faculty lot, I turned off the key and sat for a moment, looking at the red-brick building. No fence surrounded it, and the doors were propped open to catch the spring breeze. The windows were also open, and ivy crept halfway up the walls to curl around the decorative elements in the brickwork. Quite charming, and after the inner-city campus, where faculty had to use a thumbprint to enter, and students went through a metal detector, quite head-spinning.

I knew nothing about the teacher I was replacing except that his pregnancy had become high-risk, and his doctor ordered him into bed for the duration. I would be teaching a variety of classes, including world history, political science, and geography. And omega studies. That should prove interesting. I'd actually requested a woman teach that, but no one was available, and the principal, a Mr. Armison with twinkling eyes, a stern jaw, and immaculate white shirt with sleeves rolled up to show forearms that made me drool, patted me on the back, told me he had faith in me and not to be sexist, and ushered me out of his office.

I wanted to explain that it wasn't sexism, but that I hadn't taught it before and worried about having enough time to get it right, but somehow hadn't found the words before the brown-and-beige diamond-shaped floor tiles of the hallway were under my feet.

If I hadn't been so focused on his looks and his scent of sandalwood and some obscure spice, I might have been more effective in my campaign. But I would make it work. I'd make it all work.

The last day of spring break, a Monday in this district, meant no students would be around, making the wide-open school even more unusual, but it was warm for March, and perhaps the maintenance staff sought to air out the building while they could. I piled my rolling cart high and started for the nearest door, making lists in my mind of everything I sought to accomplish before I faced my students on Tuesday morning.

I had been less than impressed with the classroom decor, although the lack of graffiti indoors and out was refreshing. In the city I'd had to work hard to create an inviting atmosphere for students who made their complete lack of interest in attending clear. I'd gone home every day exhausted and returned to throw all my energy into trying to make a dent in their armor. My ex never felt that way, convinced his job was to show up, offer knowledge, and if those he offered it to didn't want to learn English, their loss.

So my tears and exhaustion were a constant source of conflict between us.

Add in my desire to marry and start a family, something he claimed he was not ready for yet—as evidenced by a brief affair with the school basketball coach—and we were doomed. I'd spent the last two weeks couch hopping to avoid going home. And this weekend moving everything into storage. Technically, I was homeless, staying at a budget motel outside of town until I found a place to rent.

But my classroom would always be home to me,

and I hoped to the kids I taught. So, instead of hunting for an apartment, I would spend today preparing my room for the students. While my contract was technically that of a long-term sub, I was in no position to complain. I'd find something permanent before the fall, I hoped.

Entering the school, I once again took in the clean, neat interior with its many displays of student artwork and awards. I would not likely be able to stay here past the spring term, since it was not a big institution and when the omega returned from paternity leave in the fall, they wouldn't have room for me. But I'd enjoy it while I could.

"Mr. Coastal, there you are!" The source of my daydreams strode down the hallway toward me, just as I was about to open my—also not locked—classroom door. "I wanted to make sure you had everything you need."

Need yes, want? I could think of a few things. "I need to go through the cupboards, but as long as the students all have their textbooks, I have Mr. Crimson's lesson plans." I paused. "Am I expected to follow them to the letter?"

"No, but if you stray too far, make sure you cover the state requirements for each level. You are probably familiar with them from your previous school, correct."

"Yes, sir, but I like to do a lot of extra projects and try to bring history and the other subjects to life as much as possible. I want the kids to know how to be citizens ready to participate when they graduate, and I find the curriculum is often lacking in those areas."

He grinned, and my blood pressure rose by at least twenty points. Always handsome, smiling, he was supermodel handsome. On this student-free day, he was dressed more casually, in a fitted polo shirt and jeans that left little to the imagination. As in, they clung to powerful thighs I wanted to bite. "We expect our faculty to share their passions in their field of study wherever possible. It's one of the keys to success we believe. Looks like you'll fit right in."

He clapped me on the back and turned to walk away then stopped. "Oh, before I forget, we need your permanent address for the files. I know you just moved to town."

Oh man. "I umm...I haven't found a place yet, since I moved so suddenly." *Damn, don't say it that way. He'll ask questions you may not want to answer!* "I thought I'd check online listings this evening."

"I see." Now he hesitated. "I don't know what you have in mind, but I have a father-in-law's apartment over the garage I usually rent out. The teacher you are replacing lived there before he married his alpha, in fact."

Chapter Two

Ranger Armison

Refreshing was the word I would use to describe a teacher like Henry. I could see on his desk myriad lists and lesson plans along with his laptop, playing some kind of instrumental piano music. He was a committed teacher, and our school could use more of those.

Though on the surface, he seemed quite the opposite of me, I knew there was a connection and I wanted to explore it further.

Way further.

When he said he didn't have a place to live, my instincts kicked into gear. My alpha instincts.

"I don't know what you have in mind, but I have a father-in-law's apartment over the garage. I usually rent it out. The teacher you are replacing lived there before he married his alpha, in fact."

Henry's eyes widened and he nodded almost too eagerly. Oh, the omega had no idea how much his eagerness turned me on.

"If that would be all right, I would love to move in." He cleared his throat as though he'd said something wrong. "I mean, thank you. Would you mind if I move in tonight? I've been couch surfing and motel sleeping for far too long."

I took in his appearance. He was the typical teacher fantasy wrapped all up in a gorgeous package. His glasses, thick and black propped at the top of his nose did a good job of trying to hide his gorgeous two-toned eyes. One was green while the other was a pale brown. His full lips made the most of accentuating his firm jawline and cleft chin.

A cleft chin was a sign of great intelligence, or so I'd been told.

He filled out his gray slacks in all the right places, and the V-neck sweater did things to this principal, things that should be handled in my office, over my knee, with my hand.

And Henry calling out my name.

"Mr Armison?" he asked and I realized I'd been in Henry-sexville in my mind. I cleared my throat and turned, trying to hide the raging boner I had already, just at the thought of him naked.

"Of course. In fact, here's the key and I will text you the address." I wrestled with the metal ring and finally got the key to the garage apartment untangled from it. "I will see you tomorrow, Henry."

"Not tonight?" he asked and I gasped. Did he want to see me already?

"Tonight?" I inquired, looking at him over my shoulder because still raging boner.

"I meant when I move in."

I shuffled on my feet. "I also own a business, and I have to work tonight. I get in pretty late. But I will see you tomorrow. Good luck. I have a feeling this school will be better because of your presence."

And with that, I left the room before I kissed him senseless and then bent him over the desk for a proper lesson.

Get a grip, Ranger. He's probably not even interested.

With all of my school tasks completed, I walked out to the parking lot and, while walking across the parking lot, noticed Henry getting into a beat-up car that probably belonged in the junkyard. He saw me and waved, and I did the same before putting my backpack on both shoulders. I waited until he left, strolling slowly through the lot. I had to lock up after he left.

Henry was watching me, the sexy little devil.

Then again, I was watching him as well.

After he finally drove out, I got onto my

motorcycle after strapping on my helmet.

I revved up the cycle and took off, eager to get done with my second job and get home. I drove the three or four miles to my shop and parked my bike right under the awning that read Principal Ink. With my bike right in front of the window where I would be working for the night, I could keep an eye on it.

"Afternoon, boss man," Mike said from behind the counter. "You have appointments lined up for the entire night. Ever since you showed that portrait on social media, they have been calling in."

"The whole night?" I asked, excited about the business, but also a little bummed I wouldn't be able to see Henry again that night.

"Yep. Your last appointment is at midnight, and it's a big one." He showed me a picture of an intricate dahlia along with a skull. It would take me hours. "Your first client is already here."

I looked over to see a young man bouncing his knee. I got that a lot, first time nervousness.

"Give me five minutes to set up," I said to anyone who was listening and went to my station. I took off the button-down and tie of my day job to reveal a T-shirt with my logo on it. Mike had already sterilized and set up my tools, so I looked over to the young man and said, "Come on. Let's get this started."

I finished up my appointment about two in the morning and barely dragged myself home. I looked up from the driveway to see Henry's car parked in my usual spot and one soft light on inside the upstairs apartment.

He was here, in my place.

And I kind of liked seeing his car in my space—didn't mind it at all.

After showering off the events of the day and getting into bed, I let my mind wander, half-asleep, to Henry.

I reached down, under the covers, to grip my cock and picture my new teacher omega doing all the things I wanted him to, but sleep had other plans. But with his image in my mind, I rolled over and fell into a deep sleep.

Chapter Three

Henry

I didn't think I'd sleep at all, between my lower body's throbbing and inappropriate awareness of my new principal and landlord and all the research I needed to do to teach my first omega studies class the next day. The other subject I'd already taken on many times and while the teacher I replaced had a solid curriculum for this one laid out, the synopsis was not my style. Lots of reading and a slew of reports, written mostly, and three tests. Entirely appropriate and completely not how I taught my classes.

To my surprise, once I unloaded my minimal items from the car and the bag of tacos from a truck I spotted a couple of blocks from school—one with a line snaking around the block that told me how good the food had to be—exhaustion began to settle in.

I was delighted to find the place mostly furnished because I had walked away from nearly everything. My small storage unit held more school-related items than personal. This would save me both money and time. Gratitude filled my heart as I walked through the one-bedroom unit, admiring the subtle decor. Earth-toned bedding and towels could easily be enhanced with a pop of color, and the living room held both a leather love seat and a corner desk where I could sit and look out over the landscape.

To my surprise, the principal lived about ten minutes outside of town at the fringes of the rural area. I would have expected someone with his sense of style to live in the urban center. Not that Roseville had much of an urban center. But it did have a few nice restaurants, a piano bar, and a gourmet candy store known for miles around. Out here, the only amenities were a nearby farm stand—not yet open for the season—and a honky-tonk surrounded by motorcycles. Not at all a place for Ranger Armison, stern, conservative principal of the high school and his tweed jackets.

Despite being tired, I stood at the counter of the kitchenette and gobbled my tacos in preparation for some more work. Two delicate corn tortillas were wrapped around chopped pork with a healthy topping of even finer-chopped onions and cilantro. Totally authentic, and a wonderful reminder of a few days spent on vacation in Baja California several years before. The memory was poignant now, since I'd taken the trip on spring break with my ex. Except he was my brand-new lover then, and I'd thought him wonderful, kind, and caring. Rather, he'd been good at hiding his flaws. And on that vacation, our first one together, he did a masterful job of making me believe he was everything I'd ever wanted in an alpha.

Looking back now, I could see the chinks in that perfect facade, but at the time, I'd been lonely. My dads had died not long before, and I had no siblings. Glad to have someone to spend time with who seemed so eager to make me smile.

With a shudder, I turned to look for the trash can and found it under the sink. Tossing the paper bag and foil wrappings inside, I forced back the memories that could destroy me. I had a new life now, had accepted my blindness to his faults and moved on.

What good did it do for me to be physically far away if I allowed him to occupy my mind? Create misery without even trying.

I sat at the desk and opened my laptop as the sun set in a fiery blaze beyond fields covered with the green mist of sprouting crops. No sign of the principal, but he'd mentioned a business he had to take care of. I brought up my browser to do some research and consult with one of my old professors regarding my new class.

What kind of business would a busy principal conduct after hours and why? Surely he made enough money to sustain a comfortable lifestyle, and I saw no signs of excess in his simple home with its well-maintained yard. Perhaps he ran some sort of tutoring service. I shrugged and prepared to focus on the task at hand. Because if I didn't, my dick was going to rub itself raw against my zipper.

To my relief, my professor, who I'd remembered taught omega studies on the university level, was able to direct me to various resources, enough to flesh out the synopsis I already had and insert some fun and enlightening activities that would make the class more meaningful to my students.

At some point, while reading about omega suffrage in the US and Canada, my eyes closed and my head dropped to the desk. I only actually knew this because when the rumble of a motorcycle engine woke me, my cheek was stuck to the smooth wood by half-dried saliva and a cloud of onion breath nearly choked me. Also, the screen was still set to a Susan B. Anthony site.

I struggled upright, listening for the bike to roar on past, but instead it got closer and closer, as if it pulled into the driveway. Images of criminal bikers from the honky-tonk flooded my mind, and I pushed to my feet, tiptoed toward the door, and peeked out through the window beside it.

The rider, dressed in helmet with full face shield, leather jacket, jeans, and boots, turned off the engine and swung a leg over the saddle. I reached for my phone then tried to remember where I'd set it down.

The rider moved toward the front door of the house, his boot steps loud in the silence of the countryside. I had to call for help, but even if I did, how long would it take for a cop to get there? It wasn't like we were right next to the police station.

The principal wasn't home yet, or was he? I'd been asleep for—the clock indicated about four hours. He probably drove some nearly silent hybrid and had parked it in the garage under my unit and gone inside his home without my hearing a thing. He was probably sleeping in his bed, unaware of the stranger who even now stood at his front door ready to...ready to pull out a set of keys and slide one into the lock.

Suddenly, the picture came into focus.

The principal had a thing for bad boys. And this one lived there. Proving once again what a bad judge I was of men. Not that this man had done anything wrong, but not only was he not available, I was not his type.

Dammit.

Chapter Four

Ranger

I woke up early and put on a full pot of coffee and popped some cinnamon rolls in the oven, fully intending on inviting my new guest-house dweller over to breakfast. But, as I looked out the window, doing a few dishes as not to seem like a slob, I saw him toss his briefcase into his car and speed out of the driveway like fire was on his tail.

In the window's reflection, I saw my frown. Yeah, the new teacher at my school was hot and I got some good vibes from him, but maybe I had it all wrong.

Maybe he was mated or in one of those *it's complicated* relationships.

Maybe I simply wasn't his type.

Maybe I was too old, and it would be weird to date the principal.

Instead of eating the cinnamon rolls, I piled them into a plastic bag and stuck them into my backpack. I would set them in the teacher's lounge and, before I could announce their arrival, they would be gone.

After pouring myself a to-go cup of dark roast, I

stuck the non-spill cup in my pack along with the rolls then got on my motorcycle and went to school. The first day was always exciting for me, but also for the teachers.

They would still have that rested, hopeful gleam in their eye.

I'd give it to the end of the day.

After that, they'd be dragging like it was the last day of school. They worked so hard for little appreciation.

With the cinnamon rolls in the lounge, I went to my office and went over my speech for the first-day assembly. I'd give it my best shot. I tried to inspire my students each year, but their iPad personalities gave most of them the attention span of a flea.

"Good morning, everyone," I said, coming out of my office, straightening my tie. I hated the damned thing, but I guessed it was necessary. Beneath this button-down were full sleeves and a chest and back full of artwork that most would never see. They'd be shocked.

I saw Henry at the front of the check-in desk and decided to take a chance. He was clocking in on our new system. I would, of course, be friendly with him, even if he wasn't romantically interested in me.

"Good morning, Henry," I said and walked up to the counter.

"Oh, hello. I have to get to class." He left without another word, and the door to the office slammed behind him.

Chace, the secretary, said from behind me, "It's only the first day. What did you do to our new teacher already? Did he park in your spot?"

I chuckled, but felt my face heat. His turn in attitude was a mystery to me. "I don't have a parking spot. Everyone knows this."

Chace answered the phone but told whoever it was to hold on. "Then what did you do?"

I sighed and watched Henry stomp off down the hall and then make a cutting right. "I have no clue."

I heard Chace go back to the phone call, and I made my way to the gym where all the students and teachers would be gathered in the next half hour.

Students said hello and good morning to me on my way, and I had to admit those back-from-spring-break jitters had me just as much as I bet they did the students.

I loved this school and prided myself in running it up to standards, above standards in most ways.

I watched for Henry to come through those doors.

When he did, another teacher, Mr. Brighton, had his attention. Henry chuckled at something he said, and a twisting wave of jealousy wound through my veins. No, I had no right to feel that way. He wasn't mine.

He isn't mine.

After my speech, almost every teacher came up and shook my hand before escorting their students back to class. In the corner of my eye, I saw Henry in the back, waiting for the crowd to disperse, I assumed.

As he approached, I had to tamp down my smile. I must remain professional.

"Henry, good to have you here. I hope you found everything last night at the apartment. If you need anything let me know. I noticed your light still on last night when I came in. I hope there was nothing amiss."

The rest of the teachers had filed out. Henry had no homeroom, so he was free for the first period.

"Oh, I didn't see you come in. I saw someone on a motorcycle. Your mate or someone to see you, I assumed."

He tugged at his collar while he spoke, and a lovely shade of red covered his cheeks.

I chuckled at his assumption. "The guy on the motorcycle was me. I have a truck in the garage, but I often use the bike when the weather permits." I bent down and purposefully made my voice low and spoke right next to his ear. "And for the record, I have no mate."

He shoved his hands in his pockets and looked down. "Oh, I was wrong then. I didn't expect…"

The bell rang, loud and violent above us, signaling the start of second period.

"I have to go, Mr. Armison."

And just like that, he was gone again.

He thought I had a mate. And that mate rode a motorcycle.

I picked up my notes from the speech and made my way back to my office.

I stopped dead at the entrance to the building. The breeze, cool and swift caught me by surprise as did the notion that came into my head.

"So that's why he was so brooding this morning. He thought I was taken."

I did a little side step before entering the building. Maybe this principal still had it.

Chapter Five

Henry

He didn't have a mate! The words danced in my brain even though I was about to teach the class I wasn't 100 percent sure I was ready for. In fact, for some reason my nerves faded into the background. Not that it was any of my business whether he was single or mated or married. I shouldn't care.

I entered the classroom along with a steady stream of kids, alphas as well as omegas there for omega studies. Resting a hip on the edge of the desk, I took in their fresh, young faces. After two or three minutes, I slapped a hand on the wood. "Now, let's get settled. I am Mr. Coastal, and I'll be with you for the rest of the semester."

I waited for questions, but although the kids exchanged a few glances before facing me again, none were forthcoming. Odd...

"So, I guess we'd better begin by finding out what you've already covered. I wrote a link on the blackboard. "If you'll bring up your tablets and go here, I have a little quiz all set up." I watched them pull iPads out of their bookbags and swipe the screens, only a few sighs indicating displeasure at my pop quiz.

A hand shot up. "Mr. Coastal, what if you test us on things we don't know?"

I smiled, glad someone had cared enough to ask. In the city, that wasn't always the case, especially in a new class where I hadn't had a chance to employ all my techniques to draw them in.

"Good question." I glanced down at the class list on my desk. Mr. Estes had made them sit in assigned seats, something I would end shortly, but for now it made it easier to get to know the faces with the names. "Ernie, right?"

"Yes. And I don't want to make trouble, but I need to keep my GPA up if I want to qualify for scholarships for college."

Several other students nodded, and I was even more impressed. "In answer to your question, this quiz is just to show me what you've already learned so I don't double up and waste your time. Then I'll give the quiz again at the end of the year—not that I'm telling you it's part of your final exam, mind you..."

A few giggles.

"The subject of omega studies is vast and interesting, and I want to cover as much as possible."

Same hand shot up again.

"Yes, Ernie?" He was either the class spokesman or would be the student who drove me nuts with interruptions, but only time would tell. Also, I wanted more of them to speak, and would make that a priority.

"Everyone knows there are only a few omegas who have been high achievers, made a real difference." Ernie was clearly an alpha, and one with some prejudices. I was starting to be glad to teach this class, wonder why I hadn't before. I might make a real difference. As long as he didn't try to take charge because his teacher was an alpha. I hoped his grade concerns would keep him in line—or I would.

"Really? Everyone knows?" Nods all around. Dammit. "You mean like the big four?"

Nods again.

"All right. Take the quiz and then we'll talk."

Roseville High, I'd learned, provided all the students with the tablet, but my predecessor had not made use of them, instead handing out printed pages for all assignments and tests. With such a great tool available, and the school's electronic grade recording top-notch, I could see no reason to waste all that paper. Not to mention that modern students, in my experience, responded much better to electronics than paper.

They all settled in to answer the questions, of which there were two hundred. I'd borrowed it, with permission, from my professor due to lack of time to make my own. But with the attitude I'd encountered, the belief only a few omegas had ever done anything worth mentioning, I had my work cut out for me.

I heard a tap on the door and looked over to see the principal's face framed in its small window. He opened the door and stepped inside. "Mr. Coastal, may I see you in the hallway for a moment?"

"Certainly, Mr. Armison." I addressed the class. "I will be right out in the hallway, so just continue the quiz while I am gone. And if any of you are considering cheating, remember this will not be graded. I just need to establish what you've already learned and what we need to cover together."

Ernie's hand twitched and I cut him off at the pass. "This is not for a grade."

I followed the principal into the hallway and let the door click closed behind us. "Is something wrong, Mr. Armison?"

"First, whenever we are not in the classroom, it's Ranger. We are neighbors now."

"Technically, you are my boss and my landlord. I should probably call you sir," I replied, taking a peek through the window to see the students being reasonably well-behaved.

His blue eyes sparkled. "I don't hate the sound of that." His gaze seemed to bore straight into my soul, and despite myself, shifted under it. And hardened. Dammit, this man was going to get me in trouble. And probably have to fire and evict me as a result. How could I remain professional when every time I got within a few yards of him I wanted to rip off my clothes and beg him to do every naughtiness he could think of?

"Henry, did you hear me?"

Damn. I'd spaced out. "I'm sorry, no."

"I asked how it's going? You were concerned about teaching this class."

"Oh." Focus, Henry. "So far so good. I got some help from a former professor of mine last night and am actually very excited now. I had no idea how limited the subject was often taught and how much more we could be sharing. Did you know the common wisdom is there are only four omegas worth studying? When there are so many! We need to show these kids that being an omega doesn't limit them. That they are capable of doing anything. And show the alphas in the group that omegas are worthy of their respect I..."

"Good god, omega, you're hot when you're passionate." His voice was hoarse, and for a long moment we just stared at one another. Then I heard a rattle from the other side of the door and a burst of laughter, breaking our moment.

"Uh-oh, looks like they're starting to take advantage." I grasped the doorknob. "Thanks for checking in." With no idea how to respond, and a real concern about my ability to teach anything if I stayed there for another second, I slipped back inside.

But as the automatic-closing door took its sweet time, the alpha's scent reached my nose. Woodsy and clean...and going right to my head. I quickly strode to my desk and sat down behind it, trying to look as if I'd just come from the most ordinary of short meetings.

It didn't help that the principal, that Ranger winked from the window before disappearing down the hall.

No, it didn't help at all.

Chapter Six

Ranger

Oh, my new teacher was interested. Not only did he blush every time I talked to him, but the tent in his pants showed me he was very interested.

And when he called me Mr. Armison, I almost came right there in the hallway next to the lockers.

So, I did what any man would do.

I put a note in his teacher's box and waited for his reply.

You know, like a fourth grader.

Henry, I'd like to invite you over for dinner tonight. Yes, a date. Seven—my house—don't knock.

I put the note in his box and sat next to Chace near the end of the day and waited. I had no sense of pride when it came to this man. I had to see his reaction when he read the note.

"What did you do now?" Chace asked, leaning back in his chair but pretending to show me something on the school calendar.

"Just inviting a colleague to dinner. No biggie."

Chace grinned from ear to ear. "Well, it's been

some time since you dated. For your sake, I hope it is a biggie and long and..."

"Shut it. Here he comes." Chace got slapped on the shoulder for that comment, though he wasn't wrong.

"So, on this week we have a conflict with the last day of school, sir." There was no damned conflict, but Chace was playing it cool, or trying to, which in itself was the opposite of cool.

"I see. What can we do about it?" I spoke to Chace, but my eyes were on Henry. He reached into his inbox and looked at some flyer and then pulled out my note. After he read it, his cheeks bloomed a beautiful pink hue and he ticked his gaze over to me.

I winked at him.

He folded the note carefully, stuck it in his front pocket, and then wordlessly clocked out and left the office.

"Oh my, alpha. You're so getting some tonight." Chase put his hand up for a high five, but I declined with my best stink eye. "What? You know it's true. That blush told the whole story. He wants the principal's paddle..." He went on but I blocked him out.

Then again, a man could hope.

After everyone left and I locked up the parking lot, I rushed to the market and picked up all the makings for dinner. My parents were great cooks and had always kept me right beside them as they fixed food for our family.

I made a simple dinner of chicken in a white wine sauce along with Caesar salad and strawberry shortcake for dessert. I put several different types of wine in the fridge and went to cleaning the house. After vacuuming and dusting what could be seen by a visitor, I showered quickly and put on a T-shirt and jeans.

I wanted him to know he could be casual in my home.

Plus, the bad-boy side of me wanted to show off my ink.

The chicken was kept warm in the oven while I waited. He was home—or in my apartment, which was now his home and had been there since I got back from the market.

I must've checked my watch a thousand times.

Setting the table became a joy that night. I placed us across from each other at my small table and placed candles in holders on either side of the center so I could see him as he ate my food and sat in my house.

33

Gods, I needed him so badly already.

Just as I'd set the forks in place, I heard the front door open and my stomach balled up in a bunch of nervous energy.

He was here.

In my home.

"Henry?" I yelled toward the front and paused.

"Hey," he said, coming through the doorway to the kitchen. "It smells divine in here."

I hung my head, all of the sudden thinking twice about mixing business with pleasure. "I hope this isn't too forward."

He leaned on the doorframe. "It is, but that's you, or what I know of you so far. I'm glad you invited me."

Oh, thank the gods.

"Sit down, let me bring the food to the table." I pulled the chicken from the pan and laid it on a platter and set it on the table. After getting the salad from the fridge, I sat across from him and plated some food.

"This looks great. You're a principal and you can cook and ride a motorcycle. What other hidden talents do you have, alpha?"

I could tell by the shock on his face that the word alpha had slipped out, but I didn't bring attention to it.

Henry could call me alpha anytime.

"I also own and operate a tattoo shop." He flexed his forearm. "This artwork is mine. A fellow artist did the ink, but the drawings are my own. That's my second job that keeps me out at night."

His eyes were on my arms now and he'd stopped chewing. "How many do you have?" he asked and a blush crept up his neck.

"You'll just have to find out, now won't you? Henry, tell me about you."

As we ate, he told me shallow things, but I had the feeling there was more. He didn't quite trust me yet and that was okay. I would earn it day by day if I had to.

We finished our dinner and he sat back, patting his belly. "That was so good. I've been living on fast food and food truck offerings."

"There's a great taco truck that runs a few blocks over," I remarked, getting up to retrieve dessert from the fridge.

"I had that last night."

I nodded and put the bowl of strawberries, now shiny with a sugar coating, onto the table along with the shortcakes from the oven and whipped cream.

"I saw you up pretty late—or early as it was. Your light was on when I drove up."

"Yeah." He chuckled and rubbed the back of his neck. "From my window, I thought that was your mate or someone you were seeing."

I put a shortcake on a plate and topped it with a dollop of whipped cream and streamed fresh berries over it. "Well, now that we've got that issue cleared up...dessert, omega?"

Chapter Seven

Henry

My stern, buttoned-up principal was also a tattoo artist, bad-boy biker, and if that all wasn't hot enough...he could cook! He clicked off every alpha fantasy I'd ever had. I'd have drooled if I wasn't unwilling to lose any of the gorgeous strawberries and whipped cream I was chomping on. Along with a tender shortcake flavored with just the right amount of vanilla.

"Do you like it?" Ranger toyed with his. "I don't make a lot of desserts, but this is my late aunt's recipe, and I hope I did it justice."

Swallowing, I wiped crumbs from my lips. "What a question. You have to know how amazing it is. Everything was delicious."

His smile made me want to say nice things to him forever just to see it. Ranger lifted a bite of cake and strawberries and slipped it between his full lips. He chewed thoughtfully then swallowed and gave me another grin. "It is pretty good, isn't it? Good old auntie." We both dug in then, no more talking until the last crumbs were gone and he rose to clear the table.

"Oh, I should do that," I protested, rising. "After all, you cooked."

"All right." But he also stacked and carried off some dishes. "But let's just leave them in the sink until later and maybe we can sit and talk awhile."

Talk? My ears perked, wondering what he wanted to talk about. After all, this was a date.

"Want coffee or anything?" He set his load down and opened the fridge. "Maybe some white wine? I have a chilled bottle here, should be pretty good."

"All right." I'd accept tepid water as long as we could sit down and spend some time getting to know each other. I felt a sense of surreality at how quickly things had changed. Because I'd met my alpha and, in comparison, my ex was just a faint, unpleasant memory. How could I ever have thought he was the one for me?

I took a wineglass from Ranger's hand and followed him into the living room. He waved me to the couch and sat down on it as well, about three feet away from me. "I thought you might have some questions now that you've gotten your feet wet?"

And I thought this was a date. Even with him across the couch, I could smell his scent and all I wanted was to be closer, to breathe him in. "Do we have to talk about school?"

He blinked at me. "No, I guess not. What did you want to talk about?"

I sucked in a breath. "Us." Because when you meet your mate, you don't want to waste time. Still, I was a little dizzy at my daring. Usually, I was only brave and outspoken in my role as a teacher. In relationships, with an alpha, I rarely said boo. Which was why things got so bad with my ex before I walked out.

But something deep inside surged up to make sure I didn't mess this up. If I didn't tell him what I thought, how I felt, how could I expect him to know? Maybe I hadn't cared as much with my ex. Probably because he was an alpha, but not my alpha.

About time I learned the difference.

"Us?" Ranger inquired, one brow lifting with his query. "What about us."

Shit. We'd just met, and I was acting like we were in a long-term relationship that needed fixing. What bravery I had fled into the selective mutism of my childhood. Years of therapy and love from my dads along with the help of some very special teachers had helped me overcome most of the challenges and to become a teacher. I wanted to be like them and make a difference. But in the most intense situations, that edge of social anxiety and inability to speak returned. I stared at him, my alpha, unable to say a word.

Time stretched out until, finally, Ranger reached for me. He took my hand, and my inability to speak became an inability to breathe. The dizziness worsened, and everything went black.

"Henry?" I was shaken, gently, and the words came through. To be clear, I didn't faint. When this happened, darkness cloaked my vision, but I never entirely went away. I was still in there, trying to control my body from far away, to maintain so nobody would know I had done this embarrassing thing, passing out like a goof. My therapists told me this was how anxiety affected some people. It sucked, and it hadn't happened often and not since I was about ten. Despair climbed onboard with all the other symptoms.

"Henry, what happened?" He slapped my cheeks gently then not so gently, until it stung then stopped. "Just stay here, and I'll call 911."

Dear god no! I scrambled from the dark place. "No, don't." I'd made a new start in this town, and I didn't want to lose my job because I couldn't maintain consciousness.

Fear of embarrassment—expressed by one of my favorite symptoms.

I opened my eyes to find Ranger close, inches away in fact. "We need to get you medical help. You passed out. Something's wrong."

I blinked back tears of humiliation. "No, at least not anything new. I should probably go."

But he grabbed my hand again. He'd let go of them, probably to slap me. "You aren't going anywhere, omega. You just had something happen, and you're not going anywhere except to the hospital so we can get you checked out." He caressed my temple. "I need to know you're okay."

I swiped at the tears rolling down my hot cheeks. "I have an anxiety disorder, at least I did when I was a child. It's been a long time since any of this has happened, but you'll probably want to fire me and forget you ever met me now."

Ranger's eyes took on a look of compassion. Not pity. I couldn't have borne that and would have left no matter what. No, he gave a nod and sat back, drawing me into a firm, strong embrace. "I've seen your records from your former school, and they were crushed to lose you. But as your alpha, I need to hear all about this. All about you. Yes, let's talk about us."

Chapter Eight

Ranger

We talked through the night and into the wee hours of the morning, which wasn't a big deal for me since I usually stayed up until all hours anyway with the tattoo shop.

He spoke to me openly and with each story, scooted closer to me so that by the end of the night, he fell asleep on my chest with not an inch between us.

Henry was a hell of a man.

Against the will of my alpha nature, after gently pushing out from under his sleeping form, I laid him down on my couch. I tucked a pillow from my bed under his head and covered him with a blanket. The circles under his eyes told me he needed the sleep, and since it was Saturday morning, it was no problem for him to sleep in.

At the very least, it did me good to know that he was in my home, sleeping under my roof, and enveloped by my scent.

Quietly, I took a shower, changed into a pair of shorts and a T-shirt, and decided to treat my omega to breakfast as well.

I headed for the donut shop drive-through and then the one at the coffee shop. I growled at the menu, looking at it from my truck window. I had no clue how he took his coffee or if he took coffee at all.

So, I did what any providing alpha would do. I ordered one of the cold brew, one of the frothy icy ones, and one of everything else on the menu.

Because I was insistent on pleasing him.

I sighed, waiting in the line for my order. I was in deep already. One night with him and there was no hope whatsoever for me not falling in love with Henry.

I paid for my order and got a funny look from the girl at the drive-through. It took me three trips to get it all into the house.

Three trips.

Henry was still sleeping. I'd seen him from my perch at the kitchen table. I wanted to wait for him to wake up, but my need for sugar and caffeine was too great.

My fainting omega.

I opened my laptop and read the news while I waited, trying hard not to look at him every few seconds and failing.

"What time is it?" I heard him say as I scanned a

story about something awful—typical news.

"A little past seven. Sorry if I woke you."

He raised his arms and yawned. His shirt lifted a little, revealing his stomach, the veins that led to his groin called to me like trails needing to be explored.

"I know I only slept for a few hours, but it was the best sleep I've had in a while. Thank you for giving me a blanket and a pillow. They smell like you."

I couldn't take it anymore. I closed the distance between us and gathered him into my arms. "It's not where I wanted you, but I felt like maybe it was too soon to carry you into my bed," I whispered and nuzzled his neck. His scent was now mixed with mine, and it did things to me.

"That would've been acceptable," he murmured and laid his head on my chest.

I chuckled. "Now I know. Also, we talked all night, but I have no idea what kind of coffee you like, so I got one of each."

He gasped. "You didn't."

I kissed the side of his neck. "Yeah, I did. Come see."

I waved toward the dining room table, full to the edges with every kind of donut in the area and just as many coffees.

"Oh, wow. I'm a simple guy, Ranger. An Americano and a plain donut will suffice next time."

I felt one side of my face rise in a grin. "Next time, huh? That sounds good."

He blushed, and I wrapped my arm around his waist, just in case he was going to faint.

I had to learn to recognize these things.

He sat at the table, at the chair next to mine, and opposed his own words. He not only ate the plain donut, but one of the filled, and a chocolate glazed.

"Just plain, huh?" I said and took the blueberry buttermilk, my favorite.

"I'm starving this morning. Not sure why."

Fine by me. I loved providing for him.

We ate in silence for a while. "What are your plans today, Henry?"

He shrugged. "I need to do some lesson plans and get some groceries—laundry needs to be done, too."

There was no washer or dryer in his apartment, so I got up from the table and retrieved my extra key. "You can do laundry here. Laundromats are icky."

We both laughed, and he thanked me. "I don't know where I would be living if it weren't for you. So, what are your plans?"

I cringed. My plans were usually work followed by

more work, after which I relaxed by...working.

"I have to open the shop today. It's my turn. I probably won't be home until tomorrow morning. Lots of irresponsible and weird tattoo decisions happen on a Saturday night."

He nodded, but his expression changed. I had disappointed him.

I continued, "But the shop is closed on Sundays. I'm all yours then. I mean, if you wanted to spend some time together."

His cheeks reddened, and it took all my self-discipline not to pull him onto my lap and kiss the hell out of him.

"I would really like that. What do you like to do for fun?"

I had no damned clue.

Chapter Nine

Henry

So…technically I lived over the garage. But I'd spent the previous night in Ranger's home. Albeit on the couch. But he'd wanted to carry me to his bed. The only downside to that was I sleep hard. Deep. Especially after an "episode." Which is what my old counselor called it. An episode.

The warmth and joy I'd experienced waking up in the principal's house, surrounded by his scent, faded a little as I returned to my apartment to gather laundry and get it handled. The rumble of his bike still echoed as he rode away. Why was it just when things were looking good, I managed to show my issues loud and clear? Ranger was very generous in giving me access to these amenities. In fact, he was generous in all things, and I still couldn't believe how lucky I was to have landed in Roseville and at his high school. I'd been pretty scared to make this move, and living in a motel was not helping much with that. Okay, it was a cute small town, but a lot of those staying in the motel were less than stellar characters, and I'd actually interrupted a drug deal on my way back from getting washing machine change at the office one night.

A lot like the city, but no less disturbing nonetheless.

My little "episode" last night was probably the result of being able to let my guard down a little. Still...it had been a long time since it happened. And I sure hoped it was a one-off. Because I didn't want to go back there, not ever.

Today my principal was working at his tattoo shop. I glanced at my bare arms and grimaced. I'd considered getting tattoos on more than one occasion, but always talked myself out of it. What if I hated the result? Then I'd be stuck with something ugly on my body, forever.

I stuffed the first load in the large-capacity washer then headed back to my apartment to spend some time on my omega curriculum. Although I felt like I'd gotten a good start with the class, I had so much more to learn. Only four omegas worth studying my ass! There were several omegas in that classroom, maybe more than that, and I had the opportunity to help them see their potential.

The onus weighed heavily until I reminded myself that every time I stepped into a classroom, I was on that mission. Helping kids to grow into strong, productive, happy adults.

Still, the place seemed very quiet without Ranger at home. I gathered another load—after the encounter with the drug deal I'd avoided wandering the motel, resulting in most of my clothes qualifying as laundry—and headed for the house again. Piling the dirty clothes on the floor in front of the machines, I opened the dryer and found that my landlord, boss...and I might have said crush if I had been that daring, had left a load of his own there.

I bit my lip as his scent along with the clean smell of soap washed over me. Would he mind if I folded his things? It seemed so intimate... But what if he wanted to do his towels and sheets or something tomorrow?

And I couldn't leave my whites just sitting there damp. They could get all mildewy. With little choice, I drew a T-shirt out of the machine and folded it carefully then another. They were all dark colors and many had graphics that related to either education—like one with the school band's name, another with the words *Read Write Repeat*—or his biker/tattooist persona. I tried not to be disappointed that there were no undershorts in there, no matter how pervy it made me feel. But the prize in the laundry sweepstakes was the last item—a black tank emblazoned with the logo: *Principal Ink.*

Was that the name of his shop? If his own art offered any indication, they had mad skills there.

As I continued with my tasks, it rang in the back of my mind and finally, in the middle of researching an omega scientist who'd discovered a cure for an obscure and horrible disease, I did a quick Internet search for Principal Ink.

The images that came up were outrageous. Fascinating. Colorful.

I had to have one.

Now.

I noted the address of the shop and headed outside. While I'd been playing online, the sun had set and the evening progressed. But it wasn't too late for the tattoo shop crowd. The small free-standing building glowed with light, and a row of motorcycles in front told me who that late-night clientele consisted of.

I parked in front of the next building and sat behind the wheel second-guessing my choice to come here at all. A social studies teacher, a nerdy social studies teacher—had no business walking into a place like that.

Did I?

Bikers in leather and denim arrived and left while I considered my choices. What would Ranger think of my showing up? I was hardly a typical client, at least of this studio. At least on a Saturday night. Maybe regular, boring people came on weeknights. Did regular, boring people get tattoos at all? Of course they did. It seemed everyone I met had some kind of fun ink to show off. From roses to calligraphy style letters to entire sleeves of images. A teacher at my last school had a jungle scene on his back complete with wild animals. He'd shown it off right in the faculty lounge.

I remembered my principal's words before he left. "Lots of irresponsible and weird tattoo decisions happen on a Saturday night."

It was about time I made one of those decisions. Stepping out of the car, I strode with what I hoped passed as confidence toward the open doorway and followed a tall, heavyset biker inside.

"Yeah?" a middle-aged woman sitting at a small table in the foyer demanded. "We don't have a public bathroom. You'll have to go to the gas station down the street. Ours is just for customers."

A glance at my cargo shorts and earth-toned T-shirt told me why she assumed I wasn't a customer. But I was.

"I don't need to use the bathroom. Dammit, I'm here to get a tattoo."

From my principal.

Chapter Ten

Ranger

I heard his voice and smelled his scent before I looked in his direction. I couldn't believe his words.

"Henry?" I called out, wiping alcohol over my newly completed tattoo—an alligator with a baseball hat on. Who knew anyone would want that?

I was only half paying attention to my client since the needle and ink part was done.

New rule: Henry couldn't come in while I was actively tattooing. I simply could not pay attention.

"Hey," he said and looked at the floor, blushing like I'd just flashed him.

I wished.

"You like it?" I asked the customer, not really caring if he did. I didn't trust his judgment since he picked out that monstrosity now on his arm.

The guy nodded, and I pointed to the counter. "Pay as you leave. Take care of my art."

That's what I always said.

I slid off my black rubber gloves and cleaned up my station quickly.

"What are you doing here?" I asked, bending slightly to whisper in his ear.

"I decided to get a tattoo." His shaky voice made me shudder to my core.

"Omega, have you ever gotten a tattoo?" I was sure the answer was a solid no. He blushed even redder, which I didn't think was possible, and shook his head. No, he had virgin skin.

It made me wonder if he was a virgin in other ways as well.

I chuckled. "And you thought today is the day!"

He nodded, clearly nervous.

"What were you thinking? Have you picked out your image?"

He pulled his phone from his pocket and showed me an enormous back design that spanned from shoulder to shoulder and neck to ass.

My boy went all out when he decided something. I suppressed a grin...and tried to shift so my erection was less obvious.

"Let's go sit a minute and talk. I don't have any appointments right now."

I said something to Brandon about going to my office. He was busy doing a straight shave and simply ticked his head at me in acknowledgement. I owned a tattoo shop, but it was connected to the barber shop next door, and there was a lounge area in between.

The social club we called it. And it was hopping on this Saturday night.

With my hand on Henry's lower back, we walked into my office. I closed the door behind me, shutting out the loud voices and laughter from the social club. We sat down next to each other on the battered leather sofa, the silence hanging heavy for a long moment before I cleared my throat and began.

"Henry, that's a huge tattoo."

He looked at his phone then at me again. "I know. You don't want to do it?"

I put my hand on his thigh. "I do. I absolutely want to. But this will take months. It would take me a week or so just to do the outline. It's a big undertaking for your first tattoo. Anyway, this is someone else's art. Would you mind if I made something for you that was mine? I mean, the artwork would be mine?"

Damn, he would be mine if he'd have me.

"You'd do that for me?"

He had no idea. "Of course I would. How about we do something small today, if you're still up for it?" I winked. "Just to pop your tatt cherry."

He bit down on his bottom lip. "I definitely am up

for it."

"How about a book or something simple? An anchor?"

His eyes lit up at the word anchor. "An anchor would be great. I need something to hold me down."

Did he realize how his words affected me? Probably not.

"An anchor it is. Come to my station. Unless you'd prefer some other artist?"

He stood, and I did at the same time. Our hips flush, he put his hands on my chest. "No, you do it."

I would so do it.

"Where?" I asked as we walked to my station and he sat on the black leather chair.

"Here?" He pulled up his shirt and pointed to his side, just below the ribs. Of course, it had to be there. This man was trying to give me a permanent boner.

I shook my head of the thousand fantasies that came into my mind. "Let's get started." I shaved his skin and cleaned it with alcohol, making sure to bend down and blow on the area so it didn't burn. I didn't have to use a stencil, as I did anchors in my sleep.

We decided on black ink, and I held up the machine and buzzed it. "You ready?"

His jaw was clenched. "I am."

Brave omega.

"First stick," I said, and then made one or two dots on his skin. "More?"

He turned his head and looked at me, piercing my gaze with his own. "More, alpha."

Chapter Eleven

Henry

I saw the shudder run over the alpha. My alpha, even if he didn't know it. Did he? I'd never been so sure of anything in my life, but my feelings weren't necessarily his. Still…the shudder transferred from him to me, like an electrical charge. His needle pierced my skin repeatedly, outlining an ornate anchor shape. I'd pictured something like the ones I saw on my cousins who had been in the navy, and had almost hesitated although I loved the symbolism for a different reason.

But this was to those anchors like cursive compared to block printing. It hurt, but I was so fascinated watching it come to life, I almost didn't care. The middle of the anchor disappeared, as if threaded into my body, pinning me in place. Grounding me. I'd often described my childhood anxiety as "floaty." I closed my eyes and leaned my head back, all my attention focused on the repeated stings as the alpha marked me. I shivered.

"Hold still, omega," he murmured. "Do you need a

break?"

"No." I opened my eyes, smiling at the sight of his head bent toward me.

"Since you're doing so well, would you like some color?"

"Yes, please." I loved being the center of his attention while he colored the anchor in a rainbow pattern then, as if he knew just the magic spell to fix what was wrong with me, he added a bit of ocean floor. The anchor was dug in at the bottom. Solid. Settled. Not going to float away. "Please don't stop."

He lifted his face and arched a brow. "You're handling the pain well for a virgin."

I started. How did he know? I'd been...well my former alpha had been unable to change that status due to some problems of his own. As a result, I'd never...

He still stared at me and my face flooded with heat. He hadn't meant that at all, had he? "Uh, well, I've been told I have a high pain threshold." Also, I am a virgin. But we didn't need to go there, did we? Some alphas regarded that as a challenge, others as a flaw.

"Yeah, I guess you do. I'm looking forward to marking you in a bigger way. Maybe soon."

Holy shit. My cock jabbed against my zipper while

I told myself over and over, *he means tattooing, tattooing.*

His narrowed eyes made me blush even hotter. He couldn't possibly know what I meant, could he? I was making every innocent remark into a double entendre. "Uh-huh." He stepped back and reached out. I blinked at his hand as if I'd never seen one before.

Could heads explode from too much blushing?

After a long, awkward moment, I let him close his fingers around mine and walk me to a full-length mirror on the wall. Holding my shirt up with my free hand, I took in the ink. "It's so small, but it's...it's beautiful." The anchor, the sea floor with a couple of tiny shells, and a seahorse so lifelike it seemed to be bobbing by on the current. "You're amazing."

"Glad you like it." He covered the image with plastic and I let my shirt drop.

"Wait!" A shadow loomed in the doorway, blocking the light from the hallway. "I want to see this tiny and amazing work."

"Axel, you know better than to interrupt Ranger with a client." Brandon, I thought his name was, the barber from the other shop stepped inside, pushing the biker ahead of him. "But since you have, let's show and tell."

"Easy, big fella." The biker, Axel, pushed back at the other man and I held my breath. Was a fight about to break out? Saturday night at the biker social hangout? I didn't have any experience with this environment.

But Ranger just shook his head. "You'd better lift your shirt and show them, Henry. Otherwise they'll hang out and torment us with their idea of a fun time all night."

My gaze flicked from the tattooist to the biker, to the barber, and then to my image in the mirror. I was so out of my league. "Uh, sure." Gently lifting the fabric, I bared my plastic-covered drawing. "Nice isn't it?"

I started to lower my hem, but Axel reached out grasped my wrist, stopping me "Oh no, you don't. Ranger, peel that cover back so we can see."

The air in the room thickened as my alpha fixed his gaze on the point of contact between the biker and me. "Want to take your hand off, Axel?" *Before I do it for you.* The words hung in the air, unspoken but clear.

Axel withdrew, but then burst into laughter. "So it's like that, is it?"

The barber also chortled. "Just give us a peek and

we'll go away and leave you two to your evening, all right?"

Ranger grumbled, but he did peel away the plastic and let them ogle his work. The skin around it looked a little red, but the detail, the craftsmanship, the art was obvious even to someone as inexperienced as me.

"Nice job," Axel said. "I wouldn't mind something like that worked into the sleeve you're doing for me."

"Sorry." Ranger shrugged. "You know I never repeat one of my original designs."

"Yeah." Axel leaned in and looked again. "But maybe something with that through-the-skin technique would be good."

"Sure. I can do that." Ranger replaced the covering and taped it carefully. "In fact, let's do it now. My next appointment isn't for an hour or so."

"All right." Axel slipped his jacket off and hung it up, revealing the sleeve he'd mentioned, almost covering one forearm. The other was completely inked. "Let's do it."

"I'll leave you to it," Brandon said. "Nice meeting you, Henry." Had I been introduced? I couldn't remember. The barber headed out, but before he left, I caught a look he gave the biker. I recognized it as one I sent to my alpha, too.

"I'm going to walk Henry to his car." Ranger rested a hand on my lower back, electricity shooting through his palm and into my spine. I sucked in a breath. "He's not used to the lowlife types who hang around here."

"Present company excepted?" Axel smirked.

"No."

As we returned to the front area, I reached into my pocket and groaned. "Crap. I forgot my wallet. Can I pay you at home?"

"I won't take money from you for my art."

I hesitated in the doorway. "But...it's your business."

He ushered me the rest of the way to the car and opened the door for me. "And how I run it is also my business. It was a pleasure, omega. I'll see you at home tomorrow. You can make me breakfast if you want."

He shut me into the vehicle and stood on the curb while I pulled away.

I'd make him the best breakfast he ever ate. I drove home, planning pancakes, French toast, and waffles, ever aware of the slight burn from the art on my side. Sure, it had hurt, but it had also been the most erotic experience of my life.

Who knew?

Chapter Twelve

Ranger

Henry made me forget all the things. Yeah, I'd told him to leave the plastic wrap on until I got home, but I forgot to tell him the basics.

I packed up two tattoo cleaning and care kits into my backpack and rode home.

The cool night or morning air hit me along the way home and kept me awake. I thought about my tattooing session with Henry over and over again. He was so willing, so eager. And my comment about his being a tattoo virgin brought a blush to his face that I was sure was indicative of his innocence in other areas.

I wanted to know him that way.

I drove into the driveway and didn't see a light on above the garage.

My omega was asleep—probably exhausted from the events of the day.

I was surprised he didn't faint during the inking. I kind of expected him to.

After showering and getting into bed, I fell asleep thinking about tattooing my man.

A knock on the door woke me the next morning.

I shuffled to the door in my pants and nothing much else and opened the side door. Henry stood with arms full of casserole dishes, and I let him in and took one from him. He was already dressed in his V-neck sweater and khakis.

"What's this about?" I asked, and then remembered breakfast. "Mmmm, I like it when you cook for me, omega. I almost forgot about this. What a great way to start a Sunday morning."

He smiled at me and kissed my cheek before setting the dishes along my table. Each one had a different thing. Pancakes, French toast, sausage, bacon, and even a fruit salad. He must've been up for hours.

"You did all this for me?" I asked, amazed.

"Of course. You did this for me." He pulled up his shirt to show me his ink, the place where I marked him.

I bent down to inspect my work. It was pinkish around the edges and a little puffy, but nothing out of the ordinary. I would make sure to clean it for him and put some salve on it before he left my house—if I let him leave. "It looks good. I brought you home some things to take care of it." I showed him the bag and then moved to the kitchen. "Coffee?"

He nodded and sat down after getting plates from the cabinets. I made coffee, loving that he was so comfortable in my home already.

I thought I could cook, but my omega could give me some competition. The French toast was made of cinnamon raisin bread, and he'd warmed up honey.

Goodness, just the food made me want to hurl him to bed right then and there.

The coffee maker finally went off, and I got us each a cup and brought the sugar and creamer to the table.

Henry's mouth was agape, and he had his fork poised in the air.

What in the world had gotten into him? I rushed to put down everything and to his side, afraid he'd have a fainting spell on me.

"Are you okay? What's wrong?"

He cleared his throat and looked up at me with those doe eyes. "Sorry, I was caught off guard."

"By what? Coffee?"

His cheeks flamed, and his gaze ticked down to my stomach and below. "No, these." With a shaky finger, he pointed at a vein that ran from my abs down below. My jeans hung just below where he was pointing, and instantly I made a tent. He gasped, but I chuckled. He had to know, right? He had to know his very presence turned me on like no other had.

"Do I need to go put on a shirt? I can't have you fainting at my table."

He swallowed loud and hard and then looked back up at me. "No, please don't."

The air became thick around us. "Is there something else you came over for this morning besides breakfast, omega?"

He nodded. "Yes, but it can wait until after breakfast. I think you and I both are going to need our strength."

I leaned down and kissed the top of his head. "Excellent."

I sat across from him again and while we finished our breakfast, did the look-away, stare-again game of new love. It made butterflies in my stomach and ignited my lust even more. My omega rubbed his feet up and down my legs more than once, and by the time my cup of coffee was empty, I was ready to burst.

"Henry, I can't take much more," I said, watching him finish eating way too slowly.

"Show me the way," he said breathlessly.

Chapter Thirteen

Henry

I hadn't wanted to eat any breakfast at all, but with what I had planned for the rest of the morning, I'd indeed need strength. To clarify, I didn't actually have specific plans, barring one.

I was going to offer myself to my alpha. To do with as he pleased. To use my body for his pleasure, and in that way show him my willingness to be his omega. My worthiness. I'd never been that kind of omega before, always been careful to keep up my boundaries even in my one long-term relationship. Sure, I'd acknowledge the alphas I'd known, been respectful, but I was generally respectful to everyone. This...this was different.

A little flirting during the meal had driven my libido into overdrive.

I wanted to throw myself at his feet and beg him to make me his. But even in my infatuated state that sounded a little overdramatic. And after displaying the part of me I tried hardest to keep hidden before, after doing my fainting goat act...who knew if he even still wanted me in his life. My alpha, if he indeed agreed to be such, tipped back his cup and finished the last of the coffee, his Adam's apple bobbing as he swallowed. My cock had never been harder.

Rising, I stacked our plates and placed the silverware on top, but Ranger took my arm and drew me to where he still sat. "That can wait, omega." He settled me on his knee and rested a palm against my cheek, turning my face toward his.

"But the dishes, it's such a mess." Even I wasn't buying my protests, and from the quirk in Ranger's lips, he was barely holding back a laugh. "Seriously."

He nodded. "Seriously, do you want to spend the day cleaning up or in my bed?"

My throat closed, but I forced a squeak through before his lips closed on mine. "Your b-bed."

He rose, continuing to kiss me, and strode with me in his arms through his home. I sensed the movement, but was too caught up in the heat of his mouth to notice where we were until he dropped me on the mattress with a bounce.

"Oof."

"Strip, omega." He stood there, tall, stern, and mouthwateringly handsome. Every fantasy I'd had rolled up into one package. The principal. The tattooed biker. The alpha. My alpha. And as I indulged in these thoughts, my fantasy alpha's eyes narrowed. "I guess you've changed your mind." He started to turn away, but I leapt to my feet in the middle of his mattress and treated him to a striptease at lightning speed.

"Omega, are you standing on my bed?" He stood straight, not a bit of bend in his spine and I knew who I faced.

"Yes, alpha." My heart thudded in my ears. *Yes, Principal Armison.*

"And is that respectful, to stand on the furniture?"

"No, alpha."

"Then why are you still standing there?"

"I should...I should get down?" God I was so hard, I thought I'd burst.

A nod of his head and I was on my knees in front of him, fingers poised at his belt buckle, awaiting permission to show him what I could do...or could if I'd had much more experience.

Truth was, that tatt session, although it hurt, was more intimate and sensual than anything in my past.

I lifted my gaze to his and he rested his broad palm on my head. "Go ahead."

It shouldn't be hard to open a belt, but my shaking fingers fumbled and I feared he'd get tired of waiting and tell me to stop. But he merely stroked my hair, softly, quiet, patient, and finally I managed to unfasten it and reached for the buttons. He wore jeans, not his school slacks, but it didn't matter. He was every inch the principal, and when I pushed the sides of his pants open and down a bit, to find plain white sheer cotton boxers—that somehow were sexier than even the Calvin Klein models, a droplet of sweat plopped onto my bare shoulder. From me, I was pretty sure. Grasping the waistband of his shorts, I lowered them slowly and drew out his cock.

It was big, and only a little curved, and the blunt head, deep red in his arousal, was crowned with a sparkling droplet.

The tip of my tongue swiped, collecting my reward before I opened my mouth wide and closed it over the salty, sweetness of him, lapping and sucking for all I was worth, proving my desire. But after only a few moments, he shuddered and gripped my hair, pulling me off.

"I'm too close," he panted. "You're too good at this."

"Who knew?"

"I don't mind," I protested before trying to get my lips around him again, but he only tsked.

"Not this time, omega. Get up on that bed on your hands and knees. Let me see if you're ready for me."

Ready? I was ready to spurt cum all over his bed just at the image of being ass up in front of him, but I did as he told me to do, crawling from my position on the floor onto the wide mattress and lifting my ass in the air as high as I could.

Closing my eyes, I focused on sensations, on his scent wrapping around me, the swipe of his finger over my slick before he groaned. "Omega, this isn't going to take long. I hope you'll forgive me."

And with one plunge, he filled me, his long sword cleaving between my cheeks and into my body, my alpha claiming what was rightfully his, what I had to give. In a moment, though, he reached around and gripped my cock in his long-fingered hand. "That's right, omega," he groaned. "I'm holding back until you spurt all over my bed." His strokes mirrored those of his dick thrusting deep inside and then retreating only to ram deeper, harder, faster the next time. My legs could no longer hold me, and I fell flat on the bed, making his strokes on my cock more like squeezes, but it didn't matter. My balls boiled and with a shriek, I spilled, soaking his coverlet and hand and my belly at the same time.

He roared, releasing me and grabbing my hips, fingers digging in, holding me still as he pounded me into pulp, shouting my name as he fell over me, his cum burning its way into me, marking me forever.

As he'd marked me with his ink on the outside.

And dammit if I didn't black out again. As my vision went black, I let out a long breath and went with it. Because this time, it wasn't anxiety. It was the opposite.

Whatever that was.

Chapter Fourteen

Ranger

After containing myself, barely, after the most explosive sex of my life, my mate had passed out. I was sure of it now, the fact that Henry was my mate.

"Oh, omega. I should be offended, yet, I am not," I sang to him as I pulled back the covers and tucked him in on my pillow. I looked down at my cock which had bumped against the bed, ready to go for another round—and maybe another. We both would have to wait. Henry was out cold.

I brushed a piece of hair behind his ear and decided to take a shower. The hot water beat down on me while I relived our morning delight.

Henry had been so innocent yet so willing.

We hadn't even discussed protection.

Would it be so bad for him to get pregnant? To have his belly swollen with my child? I didn't think so, but we should've discussed such things.

Then again, I couldn't have slowed myself down to talk even if I wanted to.

I shut off the water and walked out of the

bathroom with a towel around my waist after I dried off.

After checking on Henry and found him still asleep and snoring softly, I threw on some jeans and went to take care of the mess my omega was so concerned about.

While washing dishes, I semi-planned out our future and then chuckled to myself at my silliness.

"Sorry, alpha. Is it okay if I call you that? I never asked." Henry's warm arms wound around my waist and splayed against my abs.

I turned around in his embrace. "You can call me anything you like, but alpha sounds amazing from those lips."

He tipped his head and leaned against my chest. I rubbed his back and for a few moments, we reveled in the aftermath that we didn't get because of my little fainting goat.

"It's still early," I said and then kissed his hair. "How about your alpha takes you out on a date?"

He began a sultry trail of kisses around my chest and then stopped to pay attention to one nipple, the pierced one. He sucked and nibbled until I was ready to take him right there on the kitchen floor.

"That's not really the way to make me want to go

out," I said, my voice raspy.

"Okay." He kissed my mouth. "But, let's pick this up later."

"Deal," I agreed. "Let's get dressed. I already need more food. You wore me out, love."

The word slipped out, but I didn't regret it.

We got dressed in the bedroom, stealing glances at one another.

"I know a Cajun fusion place, a food truck. Sound good?" I asked, grabbing my keys and my wallet.

He clasped my hand, and my cock bobbed, volunteering to be held as well. "Sounds great. Where are we going then?"

"It's a surprise."

I intended to take him to my favorite spot out of town, near the spring to enjoy our lunch and in my own naughty mind, other things would happen as well.

We got boudin egg rolls along with dirty rice and a warm bread pudding to go. We hopped back into the truck, and I drove us out a ways to the spring and spread out a blanket when we arrived.

"A picnic. I've never really been on a picnic with a hot guy. I'll have to check this off of my fantasy list."

Oh, dear gods, my omega had a fantasy list.

"I'm happy to oblige you in any fantasy you want,"

I replied and tugged him down with me.

"This place is great. You must bring a lot of dates here." Henry blushed and then took a bite of one of the egg rolls.

"I bring no one here, Henry. Only you."

He smiled and blushed even more. "You're not eating."

I wasn't. I had a damned fine distraction sitting next to me, talking about fantasies.

"I will. Tell me more about you. I feel like I know very little. Did you always want to be a teacher?"

He shrugged. "Not always. But after school, yes. I had a great professor who inspired me. I hope I can inspire my students like that."

"I know you can. What about past relationships?"

I know it was socially wrong to ask about such things, but I had to know.

"I had an alpha once," he whispered and then looked out over the spring. "Can we not talk about that yet? It's difficult."

I took his hand in mine. "Of course, I'm sorry for asking. We didn't talk about protection this morning."

He nodded and then shocked me with his confession. "Is it wrong that I would be okay with having your child, Ranger? Already?"

I looked down at his belly. "No, not so wrong at all, Henry."

Chapter Fifteen

Henry

We ate, we made love, we napped, we ate, we made love...we had a weekend. And if this was my alpha's idea of how to spend one, sign me up. He never seemed to tire, knotting me so many times I lost track, and if I wasn't pregnant it wasn't from lack of practicing.

Not that we were "trying" or anything. This early in our relationship, just days after acknowledging it existed, that would be insane. Still, Monday came too soon, catching me up in the whirlwind of students and meetings with the committees that the omega I replaced was involved in. Turned out I was also the faculty advisor to a couple of very active clubs.

So by five p.m., when I was dragging my weary bones toward the parking lot, I had about enough energy to climb into my car and fall asleep. Luckily, even a home on the edge of town, in a town this size, was not very far away. Ranger hadn't suggested anything for tonight anyway. And I was doing my omega best not to be pushy. But maybe he would come by. I could rest a bit when I got home just in case.

Still, I plopped into the driver's seat and leaned my head back, closing my eyes for just a moment to rest...

Tap, tap, tap.

I jerked awake to see a face peering through my window. Turning the key, I rolled it down, blinking the sleep from my eyes. "Alpha, why are you still here?" A giant yawn stretched my jaw. "It must be five thirty or so."

"Try seven, omega." Seven at night and this principal still lingered on the school grounds. "I had a meeting with a parent who got off work late. What's your excuse?"

"Oh, I was just leaving."

"Mm-hmm." The sun hung on the horizon behind him, casting a rosy glow around his upright form, tailored suit hiding all the ink on the arms that held me all weekend. "I think you fell asleep. I think you worked too hard today."

"No, just the usual. I'm not tired at all." But an even bigger yawn gave lie to my protests. When my jaw relaxed, I flashed him a grin. "Okay, a little tired. I just haven't fully recovered from some workouts the past couple of days."

"Really? Maybe you should take it easy tonight, then. Just take a shower and crawl into bed."

Non-pushy me leaned out the window and gave him my best pleading eyes. "With you?"

Dammit. Non-pushy fail.

But as I swallowed, prepared to make a joke out of my words instead of the sincere demand they truly were, his eyes blazed with heat. "No, not alone. I think we've both spent enough time alone."

Tension deep inside me began to unwind at his words. I hadn't even known it was there, a spring so tight it could have blown at any moment, always with me. I pulled in the first full deep breath I could remember, and sagged. "I have. I missed you before I ever met you." The absurdity struck me. "If that's possible."

My principal, my biker tattoo guy, my alpha dropped to his knees on the coarse, oily asphalt. He showed no care for his no-doubt expensive slacks. He focused on me. "If it's not possible, then I have no explanation for what my life was like before you showed up. I never felt quite whole, always like something was missing, like I was waiting for something to happen each day. That never did."

"No, it never did." I picked up right where he left

off. "It seemed like everyone else was always happy to leave work, to get back to their family and their significant other but even when I was dating someone, I never felt like that. I was just as happy to work, to help the kids. Because they were all I had."

"Omega," his voice broke, his face inches from mine. "Omega, we've waited a very long time for each other. Let's not waste any more." And he kissed me.

His lips moved over mine slowly at first, just a brush then a press then our tongues touched. The tips only, a delicate caress. I'd never felt so aware of someone else. His scent enveloped me, his presence soothed yet inflamed me. Friends had told me about their mates, how it was different from just dating someone, but I'd had no idea.

And I couldn't explain it any better than they had. Not something words could express. I supposed I could say, "I would have sat there in the car, kissing him in the parking lot forever," but who would believe that?

No, turned out that once you met your real alpha, nobody had to explain what it meant or how it felt. Ranger deepened the kiss, still only lips and tongue touching, no other parts of our bodies, and still more intense than full-naked with anyone else.

"Hey, Mr. Armison, everything okay?"

We jerked apart as a group of boys approached, carrying giant soda cups and bags of chips. Ranger winked at me then reached into the car. "I got it. There you go." He rose, brushing off his pants. "I don't know how you got your belt caught in the seat belt but you're good to go."

I grinned and winked back. I wasn't sure how the school district would feel about us dating, and this was not the way to have it come out. But it would. And soon.

Because we were mates.

If the district protested, I'd find another job.

I couldn't imagine not teaching, but I'd die without my alpha.

Chapter Sixteen

Ranger

There were a million things to do stacked up on my desk, but as I stared out the window, tapping a pen on the armrest of my chair, I couldn't bring my thoughts to any of it.

We'd almost been caught this morning by a group of students.

Not only would it have damaged my career and reputation, Henry, as a new teacher in the district, probably would've been fired as soon as word got to the school board.

I had to figure out a way to either get a new job, transfer to a new school, or maybe quit and deal with my tattoo shop full-time.

Because giving up Henry wasn't a fucking option.

"I need those...um, what's going on, Armison?" Chace had busted through my door without knocking, which wasn't anything out of the ordinary, but today it jerked my nerves.

I blew out a breath. "What do you need, Chace?"

"The forms for the district. I gave them to you two

hours ago. A runner from the county is coming to pick them up soon."

I turned around in my chair, shuffled through the papers, and skimmed over them before signing. I hated forms. "Here," I said, shoving them in his direction.

"What's up with you?" Chace took the papers and sat down across from me.

I grumbled something incoherent.

"Oh, boy. You've got it bad. Why is this not a good thing?"

I pointed to my door. "Shut it."

He did so and then resumed his seated position. "Spill."

"Because I'm a principal, and he's a teacher, and after this weekend, I'm pretty damned sure that Henry will be showing the evidence of what we are in a few months. He just got this job, and he loves it. I won't ruin his career."

I'd confessed all the things while scrubbing my hands over my face. I looked at him to gauge his reaction.

His eyes were wide, his mouth agape. Great. "Are you saying what I think you're saying? My, my, principal man. You work fast."

I chuckled at his surprise. "But what do I do now? We were kissing this morning in the parking lot, and some kids passed by. I'm not sure they bought our attempt to hide it. I have to make a change."

Chace sat back. "I've been telling you for years to quit this place and do your tattoo thing."

I mimicked his action and leaned back in my chair. "It's not steady money, and with a possible babe on the way..."

One of his eyebrows cocked up. "Maybe it's not steady because you only work there at night. If you were there full-time, plus the barber place next door, it might bring in more steady money. The other guys at your shop can ink, but we all know everyone comes for you."

He had a point. I treated my shop like a side gig. Maybe it was time for tattooing to become my full-time hustle. I hadn't even made an effort to get another piercer in, and every day that room sat empty cost me money.

It would give me some flexibility once the baby came, and I could take the summers off with Henry.

Once the baby came...I was already planning on it.

Hell, I'd waited so long for the omega of my dreams to show up.

"Ranger, you're blushing."

I reached up and touched my face, feeling the warmth. "I love him already, Chace."

He leaned forward. "I can see that. We do what we have to do to keep the ones we love around, right? We do whatever it takes."

"Whatever it takes, yeah. Thanks, Chace."

"No problem. I'll go back to work now. Maybe you should work on giving a notice. End of the semester is coming soon. You'll want to give the district time to find your replacement."

A bundle of nerves tangled in my stomach. He was right. This had to be done in a timely manner.

But, first, I had to talk it over with my omega. I wasn't in this alone anymore. I had a partner, another half of me.

We had to make this decision together.

I sent Henry a text, asking him over for dinner that night. He would put up a fight about it, but something had to give. I also texted Mike and told him I was taking the night off from the shop. I had some things to take care of.

Love to, Henry replied.

He'd texted back right away, and I looked at the time. He was between classes.

The stack on my desk wasn't getting any smaller with me daydreaming, so I went about my work, trying to clear my desk before the end of the day.

"Make a decision?" Chace said as I walked down the hall at lunchtime, most of my paperwork completed. I liked to walk the halls and talk to the kids who were making their way to lunch. Plus, I needed to see Henry. He was the only thing that could quench my thirst.

Chapter Seventeen

Henry

My day suddenly lit up.

I'd been only half paying attention this morning, made possible because the students were working on projects in little groups. Occasionally a hand would go up, and I'd go over and answer a question or provide guidance, but most of the time I was sitting at my desk, worrying about what to do.

I looked at the young people in the classroom, working earnestly, and felt great pride that my methods were working so well. I wasn't a big fan of lectures, finding that students remembered things better if they had to get in the trenches to learn them. And when they taught one another, through various media. So one group was writing a play about an omega who had discovered the cure for a disease, another was working on a comic book about an omega "superhero" based on another who had saved a whole bus full of tourists from a would-be kidnapper. Sure, there was some poetic license in all their projects, but a factual presentation would accompany them.

Would I have to choose between the alpha who filled my soul and the kids who nourished it? It wasn't possible, but it would be necessary. If there were other schools locally, I could just transfer, but I only had a social studies degree, and this district had only one. I could tutor...but that wouldn't pay enough to live on. And to teach at another level, I'd have to go back and take some more courses, at least another two years.

For the first time in my life, I had everything I needed for happiness.

And I had to pick one?

I stood and strolled from group to group, listening in. Their laughter other days had resulted in complaints from cranky Mrs. Essex across the hall, so I monitored the noise level.

But how could I be upset that these kids were enthusiastic about learning?

A burst of laughter sent me across the room to rest a cautionary finger on my lips, and the group building a life-size statue of Ernie Smith, first omega to hit a home run in the World Series hushed but flashed me unrepentant grins.

My stomach churned. How could I leave them?

But how could I leave him?

Why would the Universe tantalize me with all my

dreams like this? Only a few weeks before, I'd have been over the moon to have one or the other. Now I greedily wanted it all.

I returned to my desk and my ruminations, letting out a sigh loud enough the group closest to my desk paused to stare. I gave them a wave and reassuring smile, and they held up their mosaic of a mosaic artist. Twisted in a good way.

Finally, the bell rang and the omega studies kids filed out. I had a planning period next, but planned to spend it driving myself crazy.

Then my phone buzzed in my pocket. I pulled it out and grinned so wide my jaws ached.

Want to come over for dinner?

Love to. It solved nothing, but I didn't even care. The evening glowed, like the pot of gold at the end of the rainbow. The decision still had to be made, but I drew out my laptop and opened a browser, hoping to find what someone else had done in my situation. Or maybe a career path I could step into and still find fulfillment.

Something.

At the click of my classroom door, I looked up. "Alpha...I mean Principal Armison, Ranger, what are you doing here?"

The corner of his full, sensual lips quirked. "I work here, omega. I mean Henry. Am I interrupting?"

Every cell in my body came to life in his presence. Once again, I felt that urge to rip off all my clothes and offer myself to him, but sanity wasn't entirely gone. So I didn't. "No, not at all. Did you need something?"

"You." His low, raspy tone tried my self-control almost to its limits. "But I just came in to chat. You don't have a class this period, right?"

"Right." I glanced at the screen in front of me and closed the laptop lid, my cheeks flaming. "Any particular subject you wanted to chat about?"

He came around my desk and rested a hip on the edge. "Well, since you asked. I'm giving my notice."

My jaw dropped, probably wide enough to show my tonsils. "Oh my god. Those kids. They saw us, didn't they? Don't quit. I'll go to the school board and tell them it was my fault. I lured you in and stole that kiss and you...you fought back." I thought quickly. "Or maybe you were just passively waiting for me to stop so you could chastise me. That's it. You chastised me and I..." I ran out of steam. And ridiculous suggestions.

Ranger's roar of laughter brought the familiar face of cranky Mrs. Essex to the window in the door, but her eyes widened at the sight of the principal speaking to a teacher and it disappeared. Great, what would she think was going on?

"Old grouch," he muttered. "She's got a complaint about someone or other every day. I'd let her go if she didn't have tenure."

"I thought it was just me and my kids."

"Not at all."

The sense of ease came and went quickly as my thoughts circled back around to the matters at hand. "Okay, so I'll quit right away. I don't know what I'll do but I might be able to get a job at the gas station or tutor, maybe teach one of the online programs or something and I—what? Stop smiling. Your career is tanking."

"About done, omega?" His eyes twinkled, holding none of the sadness or despair I'd expect to see from a principal forced to quit his position due to shocking behavior.

I nodded.

"All right, so just listen a minute. First of all, nothing is tanking. I've been stretched very thin for a long time, something that only became clear when I attempted to add a personal element—you."

Oh no. "I'm so sorry, I—"

But he shook his head and cupped my chin for a moment before releasing it. "Listening?"

I nodded again, clenching my teeth to keep from prattling on.

"I am not in the least bit sorry you showed up. Or that I fell in love with you."

I got dizzy. *Please, please, no fainting now! I don't want to miss this.*

"You okay?"

I panted a little, trying not to hyperventilate. "Yes."

"All right. So, I like being principal. I like it a lot. But I like my other job more, and someone pointed out that I can't run both this school and my shop and do them both well. So I have to choose."

Choosing...a lot of that going on today. I sucked in a breath, ready to continue my protests after he was finished.

He gave me a soft smile. "So I chose Principal Ink. After the school year ends, I'll be there full-time. Giving my art the attention it deserves. Also you."

"But you don't have to...wait. Are you saying this is what you want to do?"

"Yep. The district is guaranteed income, and I like that, but I knew the day I opened Principal Ink that if it did well, I'd have to do this. Someday. And someday has arrived."

I let out that breath in a long whoosh. "So you're not doing this just for me?"

"For us. And for me. Do you mind? I mean…that guaranteed paycheck would have been more security for you, too."

No matter what he said, even if he might have made this call later, I knew he was making it now for me. Or for us.

"As long as it's what you want, alpha. And my check will still be there, especially if I manage to get hired for next year….there may not be an opening."

"The teacher you are replacing has decided to teach at an online school after the baby comes. You will be offered a contract for next year if you want it. And frankly, omega, I think you like seeing these kids' faces every day. You're the best teacher I've ever had the pleasure to work with. The students adore you and when I stand in the hallway as they come out, they are talking about what you are teaching them. That's rare."

My heart soared and I stood up and threw my arms around him. "I love you so much." The words blurted out, but his lips on mine told me he got my sentiment loud and clear. The kiss lasted only a moment, luckily ending quickly enough that when Mrs. Essex's disapproving face appeared in the window again, we were standing side by side, looking at a folder on my desk.

I'd met the alpha for me. And it was darn lucky he loved me, too, because I had a feeling our bedroom gymnastics had borne fruit already.

"See you for dinner, omega." He winked before moving out into the hallway and just after my door clicked closed, the one across the hall opened. His voice carried back. "Hello, Mrs. Essex. I'll just take a seat here and observe your class."

The devil!

No teacher liked to be observed that way, and Mrs. Essex was spending so much time snooping on other teachers, I'd heard a rumor she wasn't doing a good job with her own classes.

Go get 'er, Ranger. Even tenure had its limits.

Chapter Eighteen

Ranger

My omega now spent zero nights in the apartment over my garage and all of them in the bed beside me. So, when I woke one morning and he wasn't lying on my chest or curled up against me, I sat up straight.

"Henry?" I shouted loud enough to be heard through the house. With a glance to the side table, I saw it was only five in the morning and while my man woke up early, he didn't wake up that early.

Then I heard a small sound from down the hall.

I threw the covers back and bounded past the other bedrooms and to the bathroom where the door was closed and a faint light shone from underneath.

I heard another noise and then knocked. "Henry? What's wrong, love?"

A grumble made its way to my ears, but I couldn't make heads or tails of it. "What?"

I heard him clear his throat and then say, "Don't come in here."

I pressed my ear to the door and listened, obeying his wishes but not wanting to. "Can I get you anything?"

The sound of heaving and coughing was the last straw. My mate was sick. He hadn't locked the door, so I went in and immediately grabbed a small towel and soaked it with cool water. Henry was on his knees in front of the toilet and retched again while holding his hand out for me to stay away.

Silly omega. I was on this earth to take care of him.

I put the cloth on the back of his neck and he pulled away and looked up at me. "Sorry. I woke up and came straight here."

"We have a bathroom next to our bedroom." Yeah, it was our bedroom now.

"I didn't want to wake you. It's the last day of school. Your last day of school."

He tried to make me leave while going back to heaving. "You can't push me out, love. I'm here. Can I get you a glass of water?"

He nodded and this time I let him shove me out so I could go to the kitchen. We had some ginger ale in the refrigerator, so I opted to give him some of that instead of water. I walked back to the bathroom, glass of bubbling soda in hand.

"Thank you," he said. He was now leaning against

the sink but looked like every bit of color had been drained from him.

"Small sips," I coaxed him, and he took my advice.

"Is it something I ate?" he asked and truly looked perplexed about the whole thing. I, however, was not, but I'd let him come to the conclusion on his own.

"I've been cooking for you. Nothing out of the ordinary. Besides, wouldn't I be sick as well?"

He nodded and took another tiny swig. "Maybe I've caught a bug from one of the kids."

I shook my head. "We haven't had a spread of anything, no increase in absences."

"Huh." He put the glass down and splashed water on his face. I watched him in the mirror scrub a towel over his cheeks and forehead, wiping away the water and then in an instant, he met my gaze. "You don't think…"

"I do think," I said and playfully slapped his boxer-clad behind. "We can find out, you know."

"How?"

I reached for the drawer next to him and pulled out a pregnancy test.

His eyes got wide and he stood up. "You just keep those around? Like, just around?"

I laughed out loud and reached for him. "Only

after I met you, love."

He sighed and took the box from me. "Two minutes—two freaking minutes that could change our lives forever."

I nodded. "Are you going to take it?"

He answered by opening the box and skimming over the instructions. Before I knew it, he was peeing on said stick and put the cap back on and let it rest on the counter. "Starting now."

I opened my arms and held him while we waited. He must've looked at his watch a million times in those two minutes.

"Time's up," he said and looked up at me. "You won't be disappointed if I'm not, right?"

I kissed his nose then his forehead then his lips. "Never. You could never disappoint me."

"Okay, let's look."

He held up the stick and then showed it to me.

Two minutes.

Two lines on the stick.

And now we two were three.

I put the stick down and just in time to catch Henry as he lost all control.

My fainting omega and I were going to be papas.

Chapter Nineteen

Henry

I knew, of course on some level I knew. How could I not? But while it was something I'd always dreamed of, having a family with my alpha, it was also terrifying. The morning the lines appeared on the stick, I proved my fitness for parenthood by passing right out in the bathroom. If Ranger had not been there to catch me, I'd have probably hit my head and died. But wasn't his being there a big part of why I'd fainted?

Years of work had helped me get through the crippling social anxiety symptoms of my youth, but it seemed that at least one symptom, fainting, was once again rearing its ugly head. True, it had only happened twice recently, but what if I started fainting all over the place when I had a baby to watch over?

My stomach churned and I grabbed the ginger ale glass and took a sip, only now recognizing that I was in bed and the glass was on the bedside table. Last thing I remembered, I'd been in the bathroom and...and oh no.

"Ranger, did you carry me in here?" Please let me just have forgotten walking in.

He sat beside me and smiled, but I could see the worry in his eyes. "Of course I did. You fell right into my arms. Was I supposed to just drop you on the bathroom tile?"

"Well, thank you." Because what do you say when someone carries you like that? That it's the most romantic thing you ever heard of, that you are only sorry you were unconscious and missed it...or do you apologize for weighing a ton?

Well, not a ton...but enough!

"You're welcome, Henry." He stood then. "I don't want to leave you alone, but I don't know how I can miss today. Rumor has it there's a surprise party arranged. Let me call someone to stay with you, and I'll come home as quickly as isn't completely boorish."

"Leave me?" I struggled to sit up and swung my legs over the side of the bed. "Not only are you not leaving me, I'm not staying here. I was the chairperson for the surprise party committee, and I'll be damned if I'm going to miss the expression of complete shock on your face when we surprise you."

"It can't be good for you to be running around right after fainting," he protested, but a slight smirk slipped through. He thought he was so smart! He knew about the party but he couldn't have found out everything.

"Trust me, I've fainted a lot so I'm fine to continue on with life."

"Mmhmm." He tapped his cheek with his forefinger. "Okay I'll make you a deal. You come to school, but take it as easy as possible, and then afterward we'll take you to the doctor just to be sure that you and our very tiny offspring are fine."

"Ranger, I am fine," I whined. "No doctor will do anything with an omega as early in pregnancy as me. I'm not even two months along."

"Deal or no deal?" He eyed me, so stern, so...so principal. A shiver ran down my spine.

"Deal." Because otherwise he probably would find someone to sit with me and then go off and make his excuses and come right back. "But I doubt we can get into a doctor's office on such short notice."

"You leave that to me," he chided.

"You have ways?"

"I have Chace. He can do anything." Ranger went to his dresser and laid out fresh underwear and socks as was his habit every morning before his shower. "And once we get home, we can have our own private celebration." He paused and leveled that stern stare again. "If the doctor says it's all right."

"If he doesn't, I'll go from office to office until I find one who does." Whiny, grouchy, difficult. My poor alpha had picked a fine omega. I almost pitied him.

The school day ended at noon, on this final day of classes, and my students had spent their time summarizing their impressions of me in a very detailed teacher assessment form designed by my alpha. When they were done, one student in each class would gather the forms and carry them to the office without my getting to see them. To preserve the anonymity of their responses. I sure hoped they said nice things. It would be a shame if I got fired for bad reviews after Ranger quit his job so I could keep mine.

When the final bell rang, everyone on campus, students, faculty, and every member of staff including the janitor and his assistant piled into the gym, the only room big enough to hold us all. The party committee had met last evening to decorate with streamers, balloons, and a large canvas upon which one very talented student had painted a life-size image of our principal...and which was signed by all.

I had no idea where we'd hang the thing, it was so

huge, but I knew it would make him smile.

When all was in place, Chace led a blindfolded principal—subtle, right?—in, and the whole school burst into a song written especially for the occasion before two freshmen led him to the front of the room. At some point, someone noticed he was still blindfolded, but other than that slight goof, it all went according to plan.

We had a version of This is Your Life at Roseville High featuring among others a group of former students who shared their thoughts about Ranger, some themed carnival-style games, and a cake big enough for the school mascot to jump out of. The senior class announced that over the summer they were all coming in to Principal Ink for matching tattoos. The junior class was still designing theirs. It was to be a new school tradition.

By the time it was over, my alpha was an emotional mess. He made a speech that started with, "I'd tell you all not to be strangers, but it looks like you plan to be customers…" He was eloquent and charming and moving, and there wasn't a dry eye in the house.

Just as I was wiping the moisture from my cheeks, Chace stepped up to the mic. "Before you all go home,

I wanted to let you know...we input your forms into the computer and based on your assessments, your teacher of the year is our newest teacher, Mr. Henry Coastal."

And damn if I didn't just topple over again.

Chapter Twenty

Ranger

Henry didn't get a choice in the matter after fainting twice in one day. Not only did he own my heart, but he now carried our family in his body, which seemed to not be so fond of standing up straight lately.

We took him to a doctor who also happened to be a midhusband as well. He confirmed what we already knew, that Henry was about six weeks along, plus took some blood.

Two days later, we found that Henry's fainting goat syndrome wasn't just some social anxiety—my omega had low blood sugar.

He recommended rest for the summer and some old-school pregnancy diet he said would ensure Papa and baby would be healthy and strong.

No more junk foods for this family, at least until the babe was born.

And for all his hard work on being teacher of the year, I planned a surprise for him.

"What's all this?" he said, after waking up past nine, usual for him now that school was out and carrying our babe was wearing him out.

I had our duffel bags packed, beach bags ready, and had packed up groceries to bring with us to the rental place. He'd been talking about getting away this summer, so I made it happen.

"This is a surprise getaway. Payback for the surprise party for me. We are all packed. All you need to do is get dressed. I'm going to load the car."

My sweet omega was still wiping the sleep from his eyes. "Where are we going?"

I chuckled and couldn't resist approaching him for a kiss and a cuddle. "Somewhere that guarantees rest and peace and relaxation for my mate."

He looked up at me, beaming. "The beach?"

I nodded.

"But what about Principal Ink?"

I sighed. My omega never ceased worrying. But I loved that about him. It would make him a tremendous father. "Principal Ink can make do without me for a week."

Henry reached out and fisted my T-shirt by my waist. "A whole week? Are you sure?"

I cupped his face in my hands. "I'm sure. I rented a cottage on the sand with a huge California King bed for you to sprawl out on all you want. This is for you, my heart. It's the least I can do, seeing as you've made my life whole. And now you're carrying my babe. It's overwhelming the gratitude and love I have for you."

By the time I got done with the laying out of my heart, Henry was crying and so was I. It wasn't my plan to make us so weepy, but I refused to let one day go by without reminding him how much he had changed my life.

"Okay, enough of that," I joked and swatted at his behind. "Go get dressed. I want to be in the ocean."

"Yes, Principal Armison," he said and winked at me before leaving. The winking had me wanting to postpone the beach and help him in the bedroom instead, not get dressed.

I piled all of the stuff in the car and made a list of groceries to pick up from the local store by the rental. I'd taken on the responsibility of making sure he ate the right things because his pregnancy hormones made him want French toast almost every meal.

With everything packed and our seat belts clicked, we took off toward the beach house. Henry, despite him saying that he slept well, napped on and off except when he got hungry.

"Look in your bag. Right at your feet," I said, trying to keep my eyes on the road.

"You packed me a lunch? Sometimes I think you're perfect."

I chuckled and the sound filled the cab of the truck. "Perfect, huh? I'm far from it, especially next to you."

We were sickly sweet in love, and I was swimming in every second of it.

He pulled out his almond butter and blackberry jam sandwich on the best organic whole-grain bread we could find. "This jam isn't bad. I could get used to this."

We got to the beach just in time for sunset. I checked in with the code the owner gave me and unpacked while Henry sat on the porch, basking in the sunset and fussing about how I didn't let him do anything.

After I got our bags put in the bedroom and the food in the kitchen, I went to join him. He sat on the edge of a lounge chair, enthralled with the view, so I saw behind him and pulled him against my chest. "Don't be mad, omega mine. You're doing quite enough growing our babe."

He relaxed against me and put his head under my chin. "I know you mean that. I just feel a little helpless sometimes. Let me help with some things."

I nodded knowing he could feel the motion. But just in case... "I will. I promise. What do you think about my choice? Good spot?"

He sighed and turned to nuzzle against me. "It's stunning, Ranger. I'm relaxed already. But not too relaxed."

He ran his hand up my thigh and then tipped his chin up to kiss me.

"You didn't get a good look at that huge bed," I commented, trailing my hand down to massage his ass.

"Well, by all means, lead the way."

Chapter Twenty-One
Henry

Beach sex...

Ranger had found a beach cottage set off by itself on a point with the ocean sweeping past on both sides, high tide nearly reaching the porch pilings. In a storm, I suspected it would actually come up underneath, and secretly wished it would happen while we were there, but the sun unrelentingly showed its face each morning and beamed down until the moon clocked in to replace it.

I'd dreamed of a vacation like this, but never thought it would come true. My fantasy man managed to make dreams come true I didn't even specify. Must be what they meant by mate. After a day or two of not seeing anyone at all, we got daring, nude sunbathing leading to nude...other things. On the deck, on the beach...and of course every room in the cottage. As we drew close to the start of the school year—which in Roseville remained an old-fashioned post-Labor Day date—I'd developed more than a little bump and had started to be a little self-conscious, but turned out my alpha was a pure exhibitionist. He was well on the way to being inked all over his body, and one of my great pleasures that trip was examining the artwork in the sunlight—or sometimes, when the fog didn't roll in, in the moonlight. Each bit was stunning and I remembered that while he didn't actually perform the needlework, he'd designed them. They told stories, and as I traced them, he shared those stories in more detail than even his beautiful artistry could do.

As we lay on the wide lounger, naked and sated, on day three, a helicopter flew over. Low. Like...no way could they miss the details. I started to stand but he pulled me back down, the satisfied smile not disappearing from his lips. "Chill, omega. They'll only be jealous."

Then, as the bladed flying machine whopped off into the distance, he rolled on top of me, already hard again. Before his cock plunged inside me, I managed to say, "You are very naughty."

He tsked, braced on his forearms. "I'm not the one sprawled naked in public while some crazy inked biker takes his ass. Who's the naughty one, omega?" His lips descending onto mine cut off any further comment, and I wrapped my arms and legs around him, wanting him closer to me than was physically possible. He drove in and retreated, over and over, finally grabbing my cock and stroking it, which had become a signal between us that he was close.

In the feat that never failed to amaze me, just as my cum spurted onto our bellies, his poured into my ass. Over his shoulder, a sailboat passed, a ways out at sea. Could they see us? Probably not, at least not clearly without binoculars...but the thought did give me a little quiver.

I was as bad as him.

We woke late every day and lazed on the beach, ate the healthy meals that so far had kept me from any further fainting spells, swam and took long walks on the beach, hand in hand. We collected shells and built sandcastles, drove into town for dinner once or twice. Visited the little stores run by local artisans. The days rolled into one another, and all too soon it was time to return home.

Driving away from our little paradise, I sighed. "I hate to leave."

He reached for my hand and gave a squeeze. "I know. Maybe we should plan to retire somewhere around here. Seems like a friendly town."

Now...we had been so caught up in one another, the only time we'd even seen people was while in the store and while they certainly weren't surly, we'd been one of those couples who can't see past each other. Still, I nodded. "Very friendly. We can save up." Inside, I was cheering that he was talking about something thirty or forty years out. And what our plans were. We had a future, I mean, I was pregnant with our child, but somehow his saying that seemed like a sunny path laid out into the years ahead.

He was saying, not in so many words, "Henry, you'll never be alone again." A big tear rolled down my cheek.

"Hey." He pulled the car over to the side of the road and cupped my face, turning me toward him. "What's wrong? I know it's hard to leave such a nice vacation, but..."

I shook my head. "Nah, it's not that. It's a happy tear. I'm heading home to our place after the very best vacation of my life, to a job that I love, teaching kids I adore, while I continue to grow our baby under my heart. Sometimes the happy is too big and it just comes out in tears. Have I thanked you for this, for everything?"

"Aww, Henry." He kissed me, long and slow. When he drew back, he said, "You know it's not that way. Everything I give you, you give back to me double. I actually thought I was happy before I met you, but then I learned I had no idea what happy was." He rested his palm on my swelling belly and gasped. "Did he or she just move?"

I grinned. "They know who their daddy is."

We had a few more golden afternoons that summer before school started, and he spent hours with his ear pressed to my middle, waiting for more action from our little one, who was only too happy to comply. As Labor Day approached, though, I began to worry a little. Would my alpha miss being principal?

But on the Saturday before school started, I came upon him filling a big carton with his principal clothes. All those lovely suits... "Hey," I protested. "What are you doing?"

"Getting rid of things I don't need anymore."

I studied him. "Are you sad?" It needed to be said. "Any regrets?"

He winked. "Not in the least. To everything there is a season, you know. And my season as principal is over, at least for the time being. If I ever feel the urge again, I'll buy more suits."

I watched, but as he reached for a particular favorite of mine, charcoal slacks with a gray jacket with elbow patches, I stayed his hand. "Not that one."

He cocked his head. "Why not?"

I shrugged. "Just in case we ever want to play school."

"My naughty omega."

"Mm-hmm." I fluttered my lashes at him. "I've been very naughty."

Chapter Twenty-Two

Ranger

Before we knew it, school was back in session. Of course, Henry's belly was the star of the show on the first day of school.

And the gossip about the principal and his omega teacher got around quicker than the flu.

It didn't matter. They could all talk all they wanted. The fact of the matter was that giving up my place as principal was the least of the things I would do for my Henry.

So, when Brandon and Axel from the shop mentioned something about a baby shower, I knew the act was something I wanted to do for my omega.

Henry followed me toward the door, sounding puzzled. It wasn't that he never came by, just that it was usually his own idea, and he'd actually had other plans for the day. "Why am I going to the shop again? Did you finish my design?"

I nodded, grasping at the excuse, and took his hand in mine while we drove the short way to my shop on a Saturday morning. "I did."

I had finished his design, but that wasn't exactly why I was bringing him there.

"You could've shown me at home and we would've had some more time in bed."

I chuckled. My omega was quite active in these last few months of his pregnancy and kept me on my toes.

We'd skipped over learning the sex of the baby since both of us were fond of surprises, and unexpected events were kind of our thing in life since we'd met.

I recounted everything in my head, hoping I got it all right. Brandon had taken care of the cake while Axel had decorated. Gods only knew what he'd done with the place.

I had food delivered and invited some of Henry's teacher friends.

Everything should've been in place when we got there, but I still spent the ride in a bundle of nerves.

"Did you hear me?" Henry asked as I turned into the shop's parking lot.

"No, I'm sorry. What did you say?"

He laughed. "I said, I can't wait until the holidays. It will be our first one together."

I lifted our intertwined hands to kiss his. "It will

be the best one ever for me. I love you, Henry."

"And I love you. What's happening?" The shop parking lot was packed. My spot was open, but the rest of the spots were taken. Cars even lined the streets around the shop.

"Come on."

I rounded the front of the car to open his door and take him by the hand inside. As soon as we entered, the place erupted with the word surprise.

"What is this?" Henry muttered, one hand on his belly and one hand squeezing mine.

"What does it look like?" Axel and Brandon had done a good job. Pastel balloons cluttered the ceiling with ribbons hanging down and tables full of presents and food lined the walls.

"A baby shower? For us?"

I couldn't help myself. I leaned down and kissed the hell out of him right there. "Of course for you. Anything for you."

"You're the best," he whispered in my ear and then left to greet our guests and his friends. After playing some silly games, we ate cake and food, and Henry soaked up the attention like a sponge. He sat in the middle of the crowd and opened gift after gift.

Our babe would have everything for the first year

because of our friends.

Henry held up each item of clothing and every other present for me to see while I took pictures.

My pregnant omega was the eighth wonder of the world to me.

After a few hours, everyone began to leave and give us their congratulations and hopes for an easy delivery. The midhusband was pleased with Henry's progress, and his blood sugar remained stable, thanks to the regimented diet and our nightly walks and other physical activity.

I prayed every night for a healthy and safe omega and babe.

They were my life.

"Ready to go?" I asked Henry, who had yawned more than once. Baby showers sucked the energy out of him, apparently.

"I am. I didn't eat cake." He beamed up at me as though he deserved an award for refusing cake. He kind of did.

"I'm proud of you."

He rubbed a circle along his belly. "I want this babe to be strong like his papa."

I kissed Henry's forehead. "And brave like his other papa. Let's go, my love. I'll pack everything into the truck."

"Okay. But I need to thank you for all of this later." He waggled his eyebrows.

"I think I can deal with that," I said and led him to the truck.

After getting everything into the truck, Brandon said he would clean the place up. I'd taken the day off but intended to go in that night for some appointments.

"Hey, you forgot to show me my design," Henry moaned in his sleep.

"It's at home. That was just a ruse to get you to the shop."

He smiled, eyes still closed. "Sneaky alpha."

After his nap, I made Henry some lunch, roasted chicken, sweet potatoes, and asparagus. He ate it like he'd never eaten before and then got up, but his eyes widened.

"What?"

"It's too early," he said and waivered before steeling himself with a chair. I rushed over to him and saw the cause for his concern. His water had broken, but we were six weeks too early.

"Okay. We are getting you to the hospital—now."

Chapter Twenty-Three

Henry

Six weeks too early...

As Ranger rode as fast as he could without crashing into any other vehicles, I prayed silently for a safe delivery and our babe. Also, that we made it to the hospital in one piece because the longer we drove, the more the odds of crashing seemed to grow.

What were the odds?

"Alpha, would you slow down a little?" I spoke carefully, so as not to end up making the news. Everything looked good, the midhusband/doctor said. At every visit. He was pleased with our progress and how the special diet was working out. Just the other day, he'd told us we were right on schedule with all things and he'd see us next week for our regular check.

I wrapped my arms as far around Ranger as I could, given my limitations. As in my cramping belly. What kind of a lunatic rode to the hospital on a motorcycle? Of course, what were the odds both our cars wouldn't start? And the single Uber driver in Roseville was out of town, the EMTs were rescuing someone else...and cabs were not a thing here.

So, with few options—probably just one—I found myself wondering if I'd be the first omega to give birth on a motorcycle "Oh owww..." I moaned softly into my helmet visor, hoping he wouldn't hear me and get even crazier. "Ranger, I think we'll have to pull over."

"Hang in there, omega," he called over his shoulder. "We'll be at the hospital in three minutes. Can you manage that long?"

"Since I don't want to have a premature baby on the sidewalk, I will." Premature. The word rang in my head. What had I done wrong? I didn't even eat cake at my own baby shower.

"Two minutes, omega."

Everything was starting to swim around me now, and speeding down the road, in labor, getting dizzy was a really bad thing. I dug my fingernails into his sides, gripping as tightly as I could and squeezing my eyes tightly shut in an attempt to shut out the topsy-turvy images.

"One minute." The wind carried his voice past me.

Another minute sounded like an eternity, but the thought of the too-tiny baby about to make its entrance gave me the strength to hold tight. Sixty, fifty-nine...another contraction rolled over me. Fifty-eight. Fifty-seven. I lost count somewhere, but as the cramping peaked, I opened my eyes to see we were about to turn into the hospital parking lot. At some point, probably while learning we couldn't get an Uber or an ambulance, he must have called ahead because a nurse and an orderly stood in the emergency room entrance with a wheelchair, and when we pulled up, they hurried toward us.

I thought the nurse was about to faint herself as she helped me to dismount while Ranger held the bike steady. "Sir, we really don't recommend riding a motorcycle so late in pregnancy. What if you'd fallen off?"

My alpha was now standing at my side, his hand on my elbow. "I'd never allow him to fall."

"Of course," she protested. "I didn't mean you would, but surely there was a better alternative." She paled even further and took my other arm. "You don't plan to take the baby home in some kind of side car, do you?"

Ranger tugged me closer to him. "What kind of a father do you think I am?"

The nurse's grip on my forearm tightened. "I'm sure I don't know, sir, but perhaps you should have thought of your family before you—"

Before the situation could deteriorate any further, I doubled up in the strongest contraction yet. They were coming so close together now, I only wanted to get inside so I had access to emergency equipment if the baby needed it. Wrenching free of both my captors, I plopped into the wheelchair and waved to the orderly. "Please take me to wherever it is I need to be. I'm six weeks early, so we didn't do the hospital tour yet."

"Let's go, little papa," he said in a soft voice. "They'll follow as soon as they realize you're gone."

"Whenever that is."

He chuckled. "It's not every day we see a patient about to give birth hop off a motorcycle. You must live a pretty wild life."

Me? Wild? "Uh actually, I'm a teacher, no not too wild, no." Although I had enjoyed him thinking that. "I'm a teacher."

"Oh." He sounded so disappointed as he pushed me toward the glass doors, I almost wanted to change what I said, maybe claim to be a teacher of stunt bikers, but I didn't want to be one of those exaggerating dads.

"Yeah, but my alpha is a tattooist."

The orderly stepped faster then, and his voice was

cheerier. "Well that must be exciting. Are you all covered with ink?"

"Not yet, just one little one. But I'm going to have a great big one as soon as I finish nursing."

"That is so cool. I've always wanted a tattoo. I just never can decide what kind to get."

We stepped into the elevator, chatting about the subject when a pounding of feet alerted us to the arrival of my alpha and the nurse. The orderly pressed the open-door button and they joined us, still deep in the argument.

Luckily, the brief respite I'd enjoyed while entering the building ended with a contraction so hard, I shouted and everyone else shut up.

Shut up and let me have this baby. I was so scared.

Chapter Twenty-Four

Ranger

The labor took hours. And when I say hours, I don't mean four or five. Despite our urgency in getting to the hospital...maybe even past what good sense dictated, Henry pushed, sweated, panted, and gritted curses through his teeth for nearly ten hours before our babe was born.

Tiny didn't even begin to describe the daughter that was now ours. The nurses whisked her away after assessing her and assigning her a number lower than what the books said was good.

"It's a girl," Henry whispered and then sighed, letting his head fall against the pillow.

My heart was absolutely torn in two. I wanted to run to the side of my daughter and make sure she was fine, but the other side of my heart was anchored right there to my omega.

He made the decision for me. "Go see if my baby girl is fine, alpha. I'm gonna sit here and rest. I promise not to run away."

The nurse in the room giggled and winked at me,

her silent promise not to let anything happen to him.

I hesitated once, and then he squeezed my hand, and I knew it was okay to leave. I rushed down to the NICU, and one of the nurses walked me through the procedure of scrubbing my hands and wrists before entering.

"They are testing her oxygen levels and taking some blood. She's a fighter. Hear those lungs?" I did. She screamed in pulses, and a tear left my eye. She was mine, but I was fucking helpless to do anything for her.

The doctor, a different one than the one who had delivered her, turned to wave me over. "She's strong. Oxygen levels are good. She's breathing on her own. We've got her on some fluids, but other than that, everything will be okay. We are going to need your mate to pump some milk in order to feed her. She needs that good nutrition and some time in an incubator to keep her temperature stable. Warmth means growth, okay?"

"Why did this happen?" I couldn't help but ask.

"We're not sure. That would be something to ask the midhusband. Come back in a few, and you can hold her."

If I thought my chest hurt before, it absolutely

shattered having to leave that room.

My only solace was going back to Henry.

"She's going to be okay, love. She's so beautiful." I sat on the edge of the bed and saw that in my absence the sheets had been changed and Henry's cheeks had pinked. Both of my loves were okay.

Henry took my hand. "I'm sorry, alpha mine. I feel like…"

I knew what he meant and I intended to put a stop to it immediately. "Henry, this is not your fault. And our babe is strong—they all said so. We can go see her in a few."

Tears flowed down both of our faces. It was one surprise neither of us had planned.

"I love you so much," I murmured and then kissed his forehead.

"I love you. So, what's her name?"

We both broke out in a laughter, and it healed me a little. "You name her, omega. You worked for months to bring her into this world."

He leaned against me. "How about Raney? A little bit Ranger and a little bit Henry."

"Raney sounds perfect. Can I get you anything?"

He pulled me down for a kiss and then whispered against my lips, "I'm starving."

After I ran downstairs to the cafeteria and got Henry a cheeseburger and fries, because he'd earned it, he nearly swallowed it whole. The nurses came in and showed him how to pump.

Afterward, he looked like he might faint, but this time from pure exhaustion.

"Go to sleep, my love. You've done well today."

His bottom lip quivered. "But I want to see her."

Heart—shattered—everywhere.

"I know, and you will. She needs her papa to be strong. Rest, and then I promise to find the fastest wheelchair in this place and take you over there."

His eyes drooped while I spoke. "Just for a minute."

Raney was able to come home just three weeks after her birth. By then, Henry had gotten her nursery set up and we were ready for our babe to be home with us.

We purchased a car seat with a cute preemie insert so she would be comfortable.

"Look, my love, here's your room." We painted it a light lavender and bought a gray crib. We had clothes from the baby shower, but they all swallowed our little nugget, so we had to go to the baby store and buy preemie outfits complete with hats and socks.

Having a preemie meant she always had to be warm. A warm baby was a growing baby, we'd been reminded over and over again.

Henry gave her the tour while I followed. I basked in this time.

"She's our princess. Aren't you Daddy's princess?" Henry cooed at the babe.

I wrapped my arms around his middle. "And you're my king."

"Yes I am. And you are mine."

I placed my lips on the side of his neck. "So when are you gonna marry me?"

Epilogue

Henry

Coming down the hallway after all our guests had gone home, I paused to peek inside the nursery. The tabletop Christmas tree in the corner cast a soft golden glow over my alpha who sat in the rocking chair holding our little Raney, giving her a bottle. Even though I had been nursing since she got home, I continued to pump so he could feed her some of the time. In the hospital, he'd taken such pleasure in doing that, I wanted it for him.

He was talking to the baby in a soft voice that was special only for her. I leaned against the wall outside the room and listened, peeking in from time to time.

"So Papa and Daddy are married now, my darling." He set the bottle down, shifted her to his shoulder, and rubbed her back. "Come on and give up the bubbles so we can talk some more."

She cooperated.

I grinned. Our delicate princess could rattle the windows with her little "bubbles." She could also create a hazmat situation with her other end, but

Ranger liked to keep her on a pedestal, even if it was sometimes a stinky one.

"That's Papa's girl. So many friends came to see us get married today, did you notice? But I think most of them wanted a peek at you."

I heard a little giggle and a deep chuckle, and my heart seized, overflowing with love.

"But you knew that, didn't you, beautiful girl? I'm glad we didn't get married before you arrived. Your presence made it a perfect day."

I couldn't stand it anymore, and slipped inside to be with them. "It was perfect, wasn't it?"

He lifted his face to me, eyes damp, and I hurried to his side and dropped to my knees. "Ranger? Are you okay?"

My big strong biker/principal/fantasy man blinked back the droplets and sniffed a little. "Okay? How could I ever describe the life I live as okay? We have great friends, both from school and from the social club, all of whom came here today to bless our family. The shop is doing so well now that I have time to give it, you have made a difference in the lives of so many of the kids as Roseville High, especially the omegas..."

"Who knew that class could be such a boon? I'm

just glad I didn't entirely muck it up."

He snorted and the baby jerked a little on his shoulder. "Sorry, Raney," he soothed. "Daddy is being silly, pretending he isn't a superstar teacher."

Well, maybe not a superstar... "Thank you. I have you to thank for everything." Shoot, now my eyes were damp. "I didn't even think I could manage that class, but you encouraged me and gave me confidence."

"Because I know potential when I see it." He moved the baby to his lap where we could see her little face, drooping eyelids and all. "Isn't that so, Raney?"

I shook my head. He didn't believe in speaking in nonsense syllables to babies and always made her a part of every conversation, even if she couldn't talk yet. "And then you gave me a home."

"I rented an apartment to you."

"Which I stayed in for less than the blink of an eye." I reached out and touched our daughter's petal-soft cheek with one finger. "And you gave up your career as a principal for me."

"I just told you how well my business is going." Stern principal voice crept in and I shivered a little. The man just did it for me. "So I didn't give up anything but being torn in too many directions."

I sighed. "Ranger, you're the best and nothing will

convince me otherwise." I took Raney from his arms and carried her to her bassinet.

My alpha joined me and together we looked down at her for a while. Raney TV we called it. Much better than anything on a screen. "Come on, omega, and let's get a little rest. How much longer before the midhusband releases you so I can remind you that I am the best?"

I followed him through the door between the nursery and our room, a door added just so we could always get to her in a flash. "Didn't I tell you? He mentioned this afternoon at the reception that we should, 'Enjoy our honeymoon.' Called it his wedding present."

"Then get those clothes off, omega. It's been too long."

We both stripped and tumbled into bed, within hearing distance of our precious daughter, and under the framed picture of three seahorses in a complex undersea kingdom. Two big ones and a baby. He'd painted it so I could enjoy it until it was for him to tattoo it on my body. "Take care of my art," he'd said after he hung his wedding present to me on the wall earlier that day. Our family. His art. Our love.

Book 1 in the Theta-Mine Series

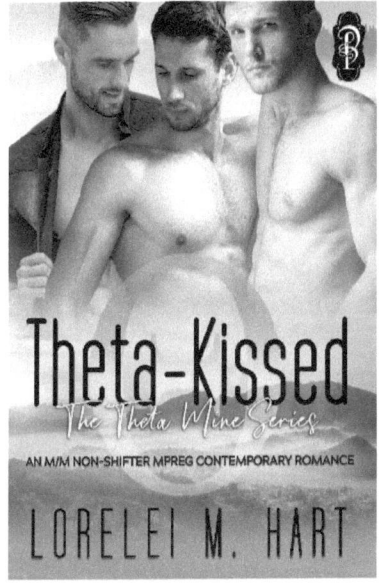

Available Here

You've never seen an omega like this.

Max travels the world as a professional YouTuber, trying out candy shops and reviewing them online. He sometimes dates, sure, but as a theta, a different and unique kind of omega, he has to be careful about whom he connects with.

When he meets alphas Harry and Kian, his theta instincts know right away that they are *the ones*, but he has to wonder—do they know what that means for their future?

Harry and Kian love each other unconditionally, and while they are living an amazing life together as a couple, sometimes it feels as if something—or maybe someone—is missing. When Max comes into The Bistro at midnight looking for a bite to eat, the connection is instantaneous—he is their third.

Coming Soon! Theta Tryst: Book 3 in the Theta-Mine Series

Also by Lorelei M. Hart

At the Christmas Inn, not all presents are wrapped in a bow.

Innkeeper alpha Miller and his mate Winston have a merry life in the town where Christmas rules. When the holiday season rolls around, people come from all over the country to enjoy both their hospitality and the wonder that is their town. Guests spend their days building snowman, decorating wreaths, caroling, enjoying romantic sleigh rides, and indulging in every kind of Christmas treat anyone can imagine. But when an emergency forces a cancellation at the inn, it opens up a room for a certain omega whose misfortunes have piled high lately.

Omega Klaus' life is on a downward trend starting with the death of his uncle, who raised him as his own. On the way back from the funeral, Klaus is on his way to a blue Christmas when he finds himself in the middle of a winter wonderland. A wonderland he might enjoy more if his car wasn't broken down, and his pockets nearly empty thanks to his mean-spirited and scroogy employer, who decided that was the perfect time to let him go.

When the towns kindly mechanic offers to find him a place to spend the night, Klaus has no choice but to agree. He is dropped off at The Christmas Inn where he finds himself confronted by two alphas his every instinct insists belong to him. But they're married to each other, and trouples are rare. Besides, even if they felt the same, what does he have to offer two handsome, successful men like them? He's broke, recently unemployed, and alone.

When it becomes apparent that all three feel the connection, it triggers heat in this guileless omega, and a night of passion ensues. In the morning, the heat is over...which can only mean one thing. A Christmas present is on the way in the form of their baby.

The Heat is On is a sweet with knotty heat non-shifter MMM Holiday Male Pregnancy Romance that takes place in a small Christmas wonderland.

Excerpt from The Alpha's Lifeguard-Kissed Omega

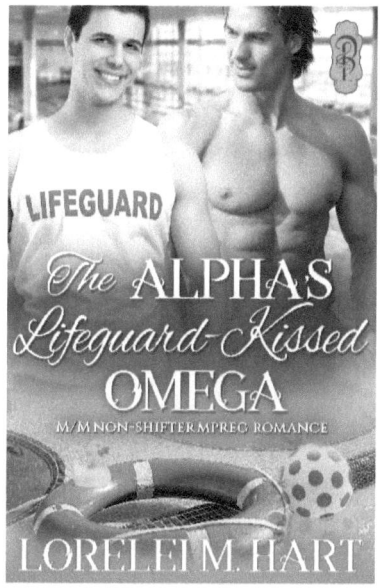

Chapter One

Luca Malone

Blowing out a breath, hoping it would give me courage, I picked up my bag and went inside the My Brother, My Sister building in town.

How completely humiliating.

A grown man who doesn't know how to swim.

Maybe David was afraid I'd sprout a tail and swim away from his wrath all those years ago.

I should have.

I saw the sign notating the entrance to the pool area and made my way through the throngs of children, running about their tasks. The place had a modern feel with computers and tablets everywhere, but alongside them books and tons of art supplies. It seemed to be the best of both worlds for a child.

The smell of chlorine hit my senses first, and I backed up against the wall, making sure I was far from the still water that seemed to be endless and bottomless at the same time.

I needed to get the hell out of here and fast.

Scooting along the wall toward the door, I looked like someone caught on the edge of the cliff, I'd bet.

"Hey! You must be Luca. I'm Harris. Nice to meet you."

A hand jutted out in my direction, but both of mine were busy, stuck to the brick walls behind me as though I'd grown spidey powers.

"Um, I'm not sure." My dry mouth could only push out those words.

I made myself look up to meet the eyes of the

sunshiny guy who was so eager to teach me to swim. Silly man, he thought my calling to make an appointment and paying for two months of lessons meant I was actually going to get into those depths.

Heavens above, I was such a loser.

"Sure you are. Come on. Take my hand."

Such sunshine.

"I am actually going to go home. I need to think about this more. You can keep the money."

He chuckled, and my insides turned to mush. "You need to learn how to swim, right?"

I did. Not for any reason in particular. The skill had been denied me in my marriage to David, and so I was pursuing all the things he wouldn't let me accomplish.

The old saying was walk before you run. Someone should've told me learn to swim and be your own person before getting married to an asshole.

Or better yet, just avoid the asshole altogether.

"Need is a strong word. I'd like to learn to swim, but it's not necessary." My words were followed by a giggle. I giggled when I got nervous, and the high-pitched sound became unstoppable.

"Come on. I'll hold your hand, and I promise not to let you drown. We won't even let you get into the pool today, well, not your whole body, anyway."

For some reason, I trusted him. Maybe it was his voice or his unruly curly hair. Maybe it was because he was the one person in the vicinity who could save my life, but either way, I took his hand and let go of the wall.

He led me to a bench where I took off my shirt and he did the same, causing me to gasp at his toned and lean swimmer's body. He didn't wear swim trunks like I did. Instead, he sported those tight, almost biker pants that left nothing to the imagination.

Nothing.

"Today, we are just going to put your feet in and talk about the swimming pool for a while, get you used to the feel of it all."

I didn't budge. Hot body and smooth voice aside, that water might as well have been a clown with an axe for all my fear.

"Luca, come on. I won't let anything happen to you. I swear."

At the sound of my name on his lips, I looked up and saw the sincerity in his eyes. He would save me before I drowned, not help to push me under.

"How did you know my name?" I asked.

"It's right here on my schedule. It is Luca, right?"

Again, my tummy swirled as he said my name. "Yes. So I don't have to get in today?"

He looked over his shoulder at the pool. "Nope. Only your feet today. The rest of your body stays out. Can you do that for me?"

I could think of a lot of things I could do for this alpha, least of all putting my toes in the water.

About the Authors

Lorelei M. Hart is the cowriting team of USA Today Bestselling Authors Kate Richards and Ever Coming as well as Ophelia Heart, another bestselling author. Friends for years, the trio decided to come together and write one of their favorite guilty pleasures: Mpreg. There is something that just does it for them about smexy men who love each other enough to start a family together in a world where they can do it the old-fashioned way.